I0535117

THE SIGNAL

by

Anthony Day

Published by Columbine Pictures Press

Copyright © 2016 Anthony Day and Columbine Pictures Press

All rights reserved.

ISBN: 0995555605
ISBN-13: 978-0-9955556-0-0

The Signal is the first in a series of comic novellas chronicling the adventures of two fiery yet elegant flappers; Samantha Bishop and her companion Nicola White.

PROLOGUE

*

With news of impending doom from across the pond and industry tightening its belt, it was enough to take the chill off a girl's champagne.

*

The train - not her normally preferred choice of transport - had left her feeling somewhat anti-social. Life was such a bore. But then she often found people such a bore.

*

But now Samantha Bishop, having spent the best part of the month shooting with her Daddy up in Scotland, was at last heading back to the gaiety of London and she was delighted to be getting back to her old routines.

*

1

She sighed silently as she took a sip, before placing the round bell-bowled glass with its delicate pedestal back upon the table. The golden liquid inside gently washed around the sides like a wave breaking on the sheer face of the harbour wall before the foaming bubbles dissolved the wave and all was calm once more. Calm on the surface but the bubbles, like the woes of the world, continued to effervesce underneath. Even if they never broke the surface, they were there all the same.

Her life was like the champagne, full of bubbles, but they didn't show on the surface.

From her small handbag resting on the table, she took out her golden compact, opened it and studied her face. Then with a tube of vibrant red lipstick, she touched up her lips. At least, regardless of all this juddering about, her lipstick should look refreshed. She snapped her compact shut with a crisp defiance that reflected her inner mood and placed both back into her handbag.

She was bored.

How she missed her beloved sports car.

She had fallen in love with it the moment she had seen one in the showroom and, although she had to wait for the coachwork to be finished, going for the beetle back rather than the duck-like one that had been on display, she had ordered one with just the same specifications.

Apart from a couple of items she had brought back with her after her years in America, buying a car that previous September, was the largest single item she had ever brought for herself.

Now she was back in Britain and, although her car was well sprung, as most the roads between London and anywhere north of the North Circular were still without tarmac and were little more than dirt tracks, she wasn't about to trade in her new darling struggle buggy for a motorbike just yet.

Nor did she want her bottom bounced black and blue over the two-day drive it would have taken, so the train had been the only option. Especially as it only took eight hours overnight.

Normally she was loath to leave London; she enjoyed the scene, as there wasn't much for her away from the city.

Not now.

Not anymore.

In her past before she moved to London maybe, but once she had started to experience the world away from her hometown of Whitstable, a small fishing port on the north Kent Coast, famed for its oysters and where the deep-sea diving suit had been developed to build the new harbour wall, London had become her adopted home.

What was it someone had once said to her? When one tires of London, they tire of life. Okay, she knew they were paraphrasing a quote by Samuel Johnson, but there again, not many people she suspected really knew the actual quote in any case. But one certainly could have a gay old time in London and she supposed when one tired of being gay, then it was time to leave London.

If she ever tired of London, she would go and live by the sea.

Anyway, she wasn't that girl she had been six years ago. Those hedonistic days were gone. Daddy wouldn't let her do those things anymore and so like the good little girl she was, she did as Daddy told her and with the handsome allowance he afforded her, she enjoyed the lavish lifestyle any young girl like her deserved.

The only reason she had left London was because Daddy had insisted. When he called, like any dutiful little girl, she came for her Daddy.

Not that she really cared for shooting, fishing or whatever else the estate offered and having to dress up to go and chase some fox across acres of country, only to get lost from the main pack and spend a lot of time, cold, hungry and exhausted from bouncing up and down in the saddle all day wasn't her idea of fun either.

Those large stuffy parties with all his business associates getting drunk and abusive around her and the intoxicating aroma of whisky and cigars mixed with expensive cologne, not something she enjoyed, made her flesh crawl. Anyway, not one of them could he really call a friend and those occasions were all so dreary. At least in London one could be free to do just whatever one liked.

One compensation though - she did like the scenery. The wide, crisp, open, blue skies, the heather-rich landscapes and the clear streams, teeming with fish and those blue-tipped mountains, she always enjoyed them as she didn't see any mountains in London. It wasn't as if she hated the country. Walking through it was fine. She just didn't enjoy living in it or being anywhere she couldn't take her Alvis.

Why he had to have such a large draughty house in the middle of nowhere was beyond her. It must have cost a godawful amount to heat. Scotland was so cold this time of year. Even though the snows had gone, it was always colder than London.

March would soon be over. The last month when it would be as bitter as it had been over the weekend and then spring and the first sighs of that fabled warm summer the press always promised.

Her glass was standing patiently on the doily, the drink inside slightly agitated by the rocking as the carriage slipped over the rails, the clattering noise breaking the normal dull rhythm as the tracks for a moment were uneven.

She picked it up by the stem and as she sipped, her mind turned to the glass.

Legion had it that these glasses where styled on the shape of Josephine's breast though she thought that was really just romantic tosh. After all, weren't glasses back then blown not moulded and even if she had posed for a mould, why? She was supposed to be the Emperor's mistress but were we really meant to believe she exposed herself for his army bimbos? There was probably a bit of mistruth about it, as most likely, one night Napoleon and Josephine were sort of fooling around in bed and just for a laugh, she had put one of the glasses over her breast and it had fitted.

A quip about maybe they had been designed for her and if he was a typical man he had probably told his generals about it and so the myth was born.

That appealed to her wicked sense of humour.

She'd done it once when she was drunk so why not? It certainly made more sense than anything history had to offer, but then that was history all over. Often the facts were changed to suit the agendas of those who wrote it, just so the story would seem either more heroic or more dramatic.

At least the train was civilised and the roast duck had been just spiffing.

She was just twenty-one and was at last a fully recognised adult now she had hit the age of maturity. She was the sign of the fish, born in early March and although she liked to read her horoscope every morning, she didn't believe in any of it. That sceptical and enquiring mind she had, told her it was all a load of junk, but at this moment, she most certainly felt like drinking like a fish. But then in her stars that morning it had said the day would turn out like this.

Of all the people on this train, she was by far the most colourful. They all blended too blandly with their single shades of mono into the rich Edwardian wooden decoration - all teak and mahogany inlays, or fifty shades of brown.

She was different, like the ornate and highly decorated armchairs they all sat on - so busily patterned but yet with depth. In contrast to her surroundings everyone else sort of fitted, but she was a modern girl, a jewel that shone bright, standing out from all around.

But there again, wasn't that the purpose of the young to be bright and gay? Her skinny, boy-like frame, dressed in a vibrant sapphire-blue sleeveless dress, and such bright red lips and rouged cheeks marked her out as one of the 'in-crowd', a 'Flapper'. She had the most piercing emerald-green eyes, with the most shockingly bright ginger shingle bob, which was poking out from under her pale-blue cloche hat and framed by her large diamond earrings that glittered in the yellow-tinged light.

From her handbag she took out her silver cigarette case with its art-deco patterned lid and, after unclipping its clasp, removed a cigarette, which she tapped on the case twice before taking from her handbag the fuchsia-coloured

Bakelite holder and slipping the cigarette into the wide end. Then with the thin end of the cigarette holder resting between her lips, she replaced the case and took out its matching silver lighter.

A quick flick of the wheel and the flint caught a spark. The little orange flame kissed the tip of the cigarette as she inhaled. The end glowed rich and orange. She let the lever go and flipped over the lid, snuffing the flame out. She then dropped the lighter back into her handbag and snapped the clasp shut in a defiant way, daring the boring people to make her conform.

As she drew another breath and blew the smoke away, she peered out the window.

It was so dark outside, the only disadvantage of taking the night train, not that the London and North Eastern Railway night train was unpleasant. The Pullman dining car itself was more than an adequate experience and the immaculately turned out white-coated porters who'd served her had been most courteous. It was just that it was such a long journey with nothing to see.

From beyond the glass it was just black, occasionally interrupted by the light of the odd city as they passed by or the brilliance of the platforms, those garish oases in a desert of nothing. But they hadn't stopped since Nottingham and, apart from the rocking of the train itself as it trundled down the tracks, the only evidence she could see that they were still really moving was the occasional way the light from within reflected off the smoke as it wrapped around the carriage.

The only thing she really could see from the window was the view from within the carriage reflected back and probably, like her, the reason most people came to the dining car or to the bar was to just have something to do. She couldn't sleep, not on a rocking train, well at least not on her own, and the night owl within her deserved some diversion just to break the tedium.

She looked about the carriage and began to notice the others, who were oblivious to her observations of them.

Behind her were two bores from Newcastle, both middle-aged businessmen, who had obviously come across each other earlier in the bar and, since entering the dining car, had done nothing but jabber on about the price of coal, the price of cotton, well almost about the price of everything from the moment the mackerel pate was served right through to the coffee and cheese course!

In front of her but at the next table there were a couple of newlyweds with the remnants of the rice on his suit and in her hair. They seemed like a well-matched couple, him with his striking film-star looks that would have given Valentino a run for his money and her, a bit demure, but with those big wide eyes constantly giving him furtive glances, him constantly on every tenth minute looking at his watch before they would lock hands and whisper softly something about nothing to each other, making her guess they had married for love.

Not something she would ever do. There was too much in her life for those sorts of emotions. Love them and move on was her mantra. Why slip a chain around one's ankle and shackle oneself to the kitchen sink when there was so much of the world to enjoy.

She also assumed they couldn't have afforded a sleeper and couldn't wait to arrive at their honeymoon hotel. Their little caring touches, their small stolen kisses when no one was looking made her wish them both a long and happy marriage. She hoped life would be as sweet to them as they seemed to be with each other. It was nice to believe such people existed in the world.

By the connecting door ahead of her, which was to the rear of the train as she always like to travel with her back to the engine, were a group of four, two men and two women, all of whom were in their fifties and who seemed pleasant enough, well-to-do fellows with their wives, she imagined, and who probably worked in the city and seemed to be drinking for it too.

She sighed and sipped her champagne, what a bore!! Although, beyond all this banality, there were one or two compensations, as, to her right across the aisle, she had noticed another woman travelling alone and this woman intrigued her immensely.

2

She was no older than eighteen at the most.

Definitely middle-class as she wasn't wearing any make-up and she was very pale, but with good poise and posture, suggesting she probably worked all day in an office rather than a shop.

Also the fact she was on this train certainly meant she had means, or at least had been able to save as no one in third class would have been able to reach the dining car.

She was wearing a green jacket with matching skirt, standard black flat shoes and yet her appearance belied hard times, as there was a slight fraying around the jacket's cuffs and, though she had on some earrings, there was no necklace or bow.

She was wearing a small sparkly peacock brooch, but that was probably paste as it didn't seem to have that deep sparkle from within that real jewellery always had.

*

Like Samantha, Nicola had left her family behind and was heading on to London, but no one was waiting for her. For her, The Big Smoke was all she had.

She was slim, had a soft-looking face and short brown hair and pale blue eyes. Though she was slightly shorter than Samantha, she sat taller as she wasn't one for slouching.

She was studying a newspaper laid out flat, reading diligently with remarkable scrutiny the small ads, looking for work somewhere, anywhere. Maybe as a secretary or in a typing pool as she had been reading the pages now for a whole twenty minutes, or at least since she had started her sweet, most of which still sat beside her in its little fluted glass bowl.

She had been reluctant to leave but, after the closure of the steel mill, her office job had gone with it and after four months of looking for a new job, she had decided to use her savings and her dole to buy a ticket and go south, to London, the city she was always being told was paved with gold and where anyone could be successful.

She had by Newcastle prices, her home town, enough money to live on for a month. The train had cost her more than she had expected, yet she was determined and knew that one of the firms in the paper was bound to take a fast and efficient secretary who could also do shorthand.

She was fluent in two other languages, German and Spanish, because of the sailors her doctor father used to treat, and knew a bit of Russian, French and Latin too.

Surely London was the place to go.

*

Samantha picked up her glass and sipped some more champagne while taking a good long look at the young woman, noticing that, despite her somewhat shabby best, the young woman had got some nice shapely gams. Firm, well defined lines and a pretty face to boot. A real Sheba, just like Clara Bow, a real life 'It Girl'. A girl she could quite get stuck on, a girl she would most certainly like to check.

A wicked smiled crept over her ruby lips as she imagined what they might get up to together, when the young woman in green stood up, a little unsteadily, and with an awkwardly tottering step made her way along the rocking carriage towards the door past the group of four.

She looked at her watch and sighed, it would be another two hours before they would reach Kings Cross Station. She sipped her champagne and looked back to the reflections in the window.

The train was a relaxing way to travel. Though she did still miss her Alvis.

*

The interconnecting door closed and Nicola found herself standing in a narrow corridor. The train seemed to be rocking more violently now, just what she didn't need, and as she winced, she took a deep breath to steady her moaning stomach. Then she started to follow the corridor, reaching out with her hands, to steady herself from being jostled from side to side.

She had never travelled so far on a train before and the speed this train was going, seventy miles per hour, was faster than she had ever been before and was beginning to make her feel both dizzy and a little nauseous.

She'd deliberately stayed off the wine at dinner, only drinking the water. It wasn't that she didn't like to drink, it was just she wasn't a great traveller, but then up until now she had had no reason to really venture further than around her home town.

Along with not eating anything too fatty or greasy, keeping everything bland but not too heavy so that it laid upon her stomach was what her father had told her would stop her feeling ill as the feeling was more psychosomatic than actually a result of the journey itself.

Your body would start to react to either being hungry or overfull. You would feel giddy from the wine and normally some simple action, such as sitting down or having a drink, would remedy most of these. However, if you allowed the train's motion to influence what was happening to your body, even simple steps like deep breathing or sucking a barley sugar, a quarter of which she had consumed since joining the train, would not be enough as the body could be fooled into thinking that these were the symptoms of motion sickness and she would still be ill.

So she had done everything she could not to let the body be swayed by the motion of the train. Yet still, even now, what with the rocking, the warmth from the heaters, the still air and the stuffiness, mixed with the stale and heady taste of the tobacco smoke, it was all beginning to make her feel queasy. Regardless of all her preparations.

She was beginning to feel quite desperate as if the next bit of rough track would be just too much for her when, to her relief, she found a door with a small brass plate marked 'Toilet'. She knocked once and waited for an answer and when she was satisfied there was no one inside, she entered.

*

The light was already on and the wooden seat was lowered, but she wasn't quite in need of that just yet.

She came over to the sink, next to the window that was masked off by a roller blind and placed her handbag by the brass tap.

She took out a small, crimson, cardboard pillbox and from that she took out one of the many small white pills she'd picked up from the chemist's whose name was embossed upon the lid, before turning on the tap.

Tuppence well spent, if the pills helped ease the acid in her stomach, calmed her nerves and eased the cramps and other complaints the manufactures claimed they were assured to cure.

She removed a small chrome cup from the bottom of a hipflask she also took out from her handbag, then filled the cup with water and, holding a pill between thumb and finger of one hand and the cup in the other, she raised the pill to her lips and as she was just about to place it upon her tongue ...

*

A little way ahead, the red and white bar signal rose; the green glass dropping as the red slipped over the lamp.

The train driver saw the red light ahead of him. Calmly, he wrapped a rag around his hand and pulled back on the lever before him and turned the brake wheel hard, before engaging the lever to its reverse position, as the fireman opened the trap to the tender and then the one to the boiler with his shovel, before beginning to shovel some more lumps of coal into the roaring fire.

The train began to slow and the wheels began to squeal as they slid upon the steel rails. Hissing steam escaped from the brakes as they bit hard upon the wheels.

*

Nicola was still at the sink when suddenly the train shuddered to a halt so sharply that it jolted her across the little room against the wall on the other side, causing her to drop the pill into the sink, and spilling the water out of her cup as she struggled to prevent herself falling onto the toilet.

The pill rolled around the basin twice before it disappeared down into the waste pipe.

She regained her feet and adjusted herself as the carriages relaxed, jolting forward and she was momentarily bumped in the opposite direction, almost falling headlong into the sink.

Steadying herself again and feeling as ill as ever, she needed some air and quickly she raised the blind and slid open the narrow, white, etched window and poked her head out, taking a deep breath to quell her heaving stomach.

She felt hot and she could feel the perspiration forming on her brow, but she was calming down with every breath and, now that the train was standing still, her nausea was ebbing away.

She took a piece of tissue paper from the holder by the sink and dabbed her brow as she let the cool air stroke her pallor away.

She was peering out into the darkness to see if she could tell why they'd stopped when she noticed not too far away there was a light coming from an office window in the middle of what was a large red-brick factory in a row of what looked like many factories in a city of similar factories, silhouetted before the dark night sky and illuminated by the low hunter's moon that looked as if it was resting upon their steep pitched roofs, trapped in place by their tall furnace chimneys, which were gently smoking as the fires within them rested, the smouldering embers keeping them ready for when the next day's frantic shift would begin.

She was drawn to the window, like a moth to a flame, its warming yellow glow seemed inviting and she began to feel happy to be at last amongst some industry. It meant they were near to a city, maybe even the outskirts of London itself and soon this nightmare journey would be over and then the real nightmare would begin, as there wasn't a soul in the whole metropolis she would be able to call upon as a friend.

A small pang of regret began to creep over her as she began to remember her beloved Newcastle, her home, her family, her three brothers, mother and father and friends, the girls she had been to school with and known all her life, that familiarity of the life she was leaving behind.

It had been a hard decision for her to leave her parents and seek a job down south, but in the recent years, things had started to get tight. Her father was as busy as ever but his patients were not always able to pay him for his time and that was making life hard at home.

They hadn't been forced yet to buy horsemeat regularly or go to the soup kitchen, but unless something changed soon, 1928 was destined to end as a really bad year. One consolation, it couldn't get any worse! With a million men already out of work, she doubted if the government would let it grow any higher or the country would never truly recover.

At least her leaving would mean that her younger brother would have a better life. Leaving home meant one less mouth to feed, which after losing her job had made the housekeeping budget tight, and he was a bright child, doing well at school. If she could make some money and send it home he would be able to go to college and become a doctor or an accountant.

That's why leaving had been the right thing to do. If working so far away in such a hostile city made her life a misery, so be it, she would do it for him.

It wasn't as if she could just go back. She would need a job just to pay for the rail ticket. She didn't even have enough for third class.

She still had to find lodgings, food and then a job before the few pounds she had left in her purse ran out.

She was shaken from her thoughts when she noticed somebody move in the factory's office window.

She watched as the figure was joined by a second and the two silhouettes lit from behind seemed to be talking with wild gesticulations when suddenly one of the silhouettes put their hands around the other's neck.

She was shocked and quickly took another pill, just as the first silhouette, the shorter of the two began to hit the second silhouette with what to her looked an axe.

A nervous panic gripped her as she took her hipflask out of her handbag and whipped off the screw top quickly to take a sip, just as the first silhouette placed what seemed to be a noose around the second silhouette's neck.

Taking a mouthful of pills and then washing them all down from the hipflask, she watched in horror as the windows were smashed by the second silhouette being thrown through them by the first.

*

The signal dropped, the red glass replaced by the green and as the driver spun the wheel back the other way and then pushed the lever forward, the engine's wheels began to spin over the steel rails, the steam from the funnel began to billow, then, as the friction bit, the engine began to slowly pull the train.

*

She was slammed against the other wall, the last of her pills showered her as she pulled herself up and, straightening herself, she looked out the window.

In the light of the passing carriages, she could see the factory sign, bold and picked out in black and gold.

BARLOW AND SONS LTD.
RUBBER
MANUFACTURERS.

3

Samantha rested her cigarette carefully on the side of the ashtray next to the small silver vase in which the single lilac flower drooped slightly towards her as she then took another sip of her champagne.

With a glance over to the table opposite and with a quick look at that open newspaper, she began to feel a slight regret she hadn't insisted the waiter moved her over to the same table when, suddenly, her dreaming was interrupted by a loud commotion as the carriage door was flung open as the young woman crashed in, the ghostly pallor of shock still upon her face as she staggered, as if drunk, almost knocking into the party of four.

Samantha picked up her cigarette and took another long drag. A pang of pity suddenly seemed to overcome her as she could see that this young woman was in distress.

'Did you see that?!!' The young woman called out to everyone but no one in particular. She had a coarse, thick northern accent and everyone in the dining car turned and looked at her, aghast at such a boisterous outburst, as the young woman pointed out towards the window on the left side of the car.

Everyone remained silent, almost to the point of ignoring her, even the two business bores behind Samantha had gone all quiet.

'Out there!' She demanded them to take notice, but the carriage remained blankly staring at her. 'Did you see it? A man being murdered!'

'Oh, I say!' remarked one of the businessmen as if the news was souring his brandy.

'I saw it! A murder!!' she insisted. Then, before anyone could stop her, she reached across the romantic couple and pulled the emergency cord.

The train shuddered to a halt, as the high-pitched squeal of the locking wheels sliding over rail echoed through the carriage, glasses and cutlery toppling as the whole train shuddered and skidded to a stop.

Much to Samantha's immediate annoyance, her champagne had spilt all over her table and she had to shift quickly, so as not to be soaked by its dribbling waterfall.

The young woman had almost fallen on top of the honeymooners. Recovering her composure, she pleaded to them all.

'Will someone help me?! Call the police?!'

The door at the opposite end opened and the guard entered, adjusting his cap as he did so. With a face like thunder, he stormed along the aisle towards the young woman.

'Who pulled the cord?' he demanded, passing by Samantha who found herself impulsively standing and following him as the young woman turned to the guard.

'I saw a man fall from a window,' she told him. He took his notebook from his jacket pocket, his mood turning from anger to concern as he replied,

'My word, that is serious! Do you know which compartment he was in?'

'Not from the train. Out there!' she replied, pointing again outside the train.

'Then there's not a lot I can do about that, miss,' the guard continued, as he noticed the faint smell of brandy on her breath. 'Unless the man was on the train, it is the rules you see, miss. L.N.E.R policy is to only consider the murder of people on our trains as important. Of anyone who's not a paying customer, that's someone else's problem. I mean, if we were to hold up the train every time there was a crime we'd be stopping and starting all along the track! Now unless there is a murder happening on this train, or anything else serious happening on this train, I must warn you that there is a fine for the improper use of pulling the communication cord.'

'But I saw a murder!' she protested vehemently.

'But he wasn't on this train,' he reminded her as he licked the tip of his pencil.

'No. But...!' She was flummoxed, she couldn't think of anything else to say and was unable to get any sympathy from the guard as he continued.

'Then this was an improper use of the communications cord and I'm afraid, miss, I'm going to have to have your name and address.'

'But...' She looked around at all the other prying eyes, the shame beginning to dawn upon her, as she admitted, 'I'm just moving down to London, looking for work!?'

A few disapproving 'mutters' drifted about the carriage, but Samantha, on seeing those beautiful pale blue eyes near to tears, tapped the guard upon the shoulder and, after blowing some smoke casually in his general direction, asked him, 'Look here, my good man. May I be of some assistance?'

'Who are you?' he asked, determined not to splutter under her cloud of smoke.

'Samantha Bishop. Here's my card.' She took from the wallet inside her handbag a card and handed it to him. She looked at the young woman and as their eyes met a tingling shimmer seemed to tremble down her spine, a warming glow beginning to invade her heart.

'I can vouch for the young lady.' she told him, snapping her handbag shut so fast he could feel the wind from it upon his cheek. 'I'm in berth 27, Lucille, if you require me any further.'

'If you're sure. The fine could be as high as ten pounds,' he replied, looking at the address on the card.

The young woman shivered with fear. Samantha could see ten pounds was a lot to her, but to herself, what was ten pounds! Daddy spent that much on cigars every day. Why, it wasn't beyond her to spend that much at the club, or even on a new pair of shoes or an outfit in a day.

'That's perfectly all right my good man.' She brushed him away and blew some more smoke in his general direction. 'Shall we get this train going again?'

The guard gave her a little nod and salute then headed back up the carriage towards the engine.

Petty bureaucrats made life such a pain at times, Samantha thought to herself.

The young woman, somewhat subdued, followed Samantha back to her seat and, as they sat together either side of the table, Samantha picked up her broken champagne glass. A mild disappointment swept over her as she had been enjoying that vintage, but when she looked up again and gazed into those pale blue eyes, she realised she didn't care anymore.

'You're going to think me a frightful nincompoop?' The young woman broke the silence as with a sudden jerk the train was moving again.

'Not at all.' Samantha replied. 'We haven't been properly introduced.'

'Sorry, no, how remiss of me. You acting like my knight in shining armour and all,' she replied with a nervous smile and then added. 'Nicola White.'

They shook hands.

'Well, Miss White, when we get to the station, let's find ourselves a constable shall we?' And for the first time since Samantha had noticed her, Nicola began to relax, her face radiating the warmest and widest smile Samantha had ever seen.

'I see you've been looking in the paper?' Samantha nodded across the aisle to where Nicola had been sitting.

'For a situation, yes. Are you just visiting London?'

'No. I live there.'

'I hope not near the centre?' Nicola remarked tentatively.

'Fortunately not!' Samantha agreed adding 'Well, not near enough to Chelsea to get my feet wet, though it should be sorted by now. That was in January!'

'I couldn't help feeling for the poor in Lambeth.' Nicola continued with a solemn tone to her words. 'What was it? Fourteen drowned in their basement flats and another four thousand homeless. Who would have thought even a heavy snow melting during an abnormally wet winter and a spring tide would do all this?'

'Quite!'

'Do you think it will ever be so bad again?'

'Well, Parliament was flooded so I expect they'll spend all the money it takes to prevent it!' Samantha replied and took a long drag on her cigarette. 'The rich would when it's their feet that get wet.'

4

The swirls of smoke disappeared up into the high glass roof, supported by ornate ironwork with its intricate leaf filigree.

With the shrieking noise of the steam whistles, the choking taste of the bitter steam, the smell of coal and the sparks from the chimneys, the engines came to life as they pulled away from the black platforms. All around, drifting through every hole and crevice, their smoke wafted past the apple and cream coloured wood and over the waiting rooms and ticket gates and up high, higher than the station clock at the far end of the concourse.

There weren't that many people about. Most of the activity around the station was people working, moving goods onto the trains, some taking goods off with their flat barrows, stacked higher than they could see over.

Everything from newspapers and cases of meat, fish, vegetables, was being loaded onto the trucks and vans to be taken to the city's various markets.

It was a hive of activity and the noise which erupted was like the underscore of an orchestra's melody, harsh and brash like much of the language the workers used to each other.

On the concourse, away from the platforms and near the entrance, there was a vendor's stall selling hot drinks and pies. It was a long, red wagon, on four wheels, with ornate paintwork around its opened-out counter announcing the trader's name as well as the produce he sold, the prices of which were chalked up next to the item.

On the counter there were a number of bottles, some for brown and red sauce, mustard, salt and vinegar as well as a bowl for sugar, which had a spoon sitting in it, and a tall enamel jug in which there was milk. The rest of the side of the wagon opened out like a metal awning and from the wagon there was a welcoming smell of frying onions and bacon wafting through the bitter smell of the engines' smoke.

Samantha was now wrapped in her sapphire-blue spring coat with the deep fur collar and holding a slightly chipped mug of tea. She stood with Nicola with her mug of coffee and Detective Inspector Marriot and two police constables, resplendent with their tall domed hats, so tall, so dominant, reassuringly recognisable for being so distinctive that just seeing them made her feel safe.

Detective Inspector Marriot was a tall man with a square, chiselled jaw, deep-set eyes and dark brown hair, which though cut short, still poked out from under his grey trilby. His hands were thrust deep into his trench-coat pockets. He spoke with an air of mild disinterest which matched his overall mood.

'And you say you saw the man fall from the window?' He hated working late, especially when he could have been home with his hot cocoa listening to the 2LO, which reminded him his radio licence was due and that just added to his foul mood.

'He was thrown, yes,' Nicola replied.

'Well, missy, if you can remember the name of the factory where you saw it happen. That is to say, there are quite a few of them along that part of the line.'

'Oh, oh, of course, Detective Inspector. Let me see....' Nicola struggled to recall. The shock of seeing a man fall from the window along with her travel sickness had been enough to confuse her. 'I think it was. Barker, no, Breaker, Bowler.' She sighed, trying hard to remember, adding, 'Oh, it all happened oh so fast!'

'Barlow?' he asked.

'Yes, that was it, Detective Inspector. Barlow's.' She smiled as Detective Inspector Marriot turned to one of the constables and nodded to him. He watched him for a moment as he headed over to the police call box, a small blue cabinet upon a blue pedestal with a light on top. Using his key, he opened it and picked up the candlestick phone from inside.

Detective Inspector Marriot turned back to both Samantha and Nicola and with a gentle but well-practised friendly smile said reassuringly, 'Now then, missy, don't you worry your poor little pretty head, we'll soon have those bad men behind bars, don't you worry.'

'Thank you.' Nicola replied, relieved things were at last happening and that someone in authority was taking her seriously.

'Now, where are you staying? In case we need to speak to you again for any reason.'

'Well, I haven't secured a place to stay as yet, Detective Inspector. I've just travelled down from Newcastle looking for a situation in town.'

'You're a little late to find a hotel room tonight, missy.'

'That's all right, Detective Inspector,' Samantha interrupted. 'She can stay with me.' She handed a card from her handbag to the Detective Inspector.

'With you?' Nicola was surprised. It already felt as if Samantha had done far too much for her as it was. She wasn't used to complete strangers taking such an interest in her. But she was glad she had. The idea of sleeping on a park bench under a blanket of newspapers didn't appeal to her.

'Yes, I don't live too far away and I have a spare room.' she told the Detective Inspector. Then with a sweet smile she turned to Nicola adding. 'It has a lock on the door, if you're worried.'

'Oh yes?' Detective Inspector Marriot raised an eyebrow. Samantha turned back to him as she replied,

'Oh yes, Detective Inspector. Sometimes my chum Geordie Bum Fluff likes to stay over when he's in town, but he's up in Scotland with his Ma, bagging a few birds.'

'Is that where you've been, Miss Bishop?' He put the card away into his coat pocket.

'Oh, bagging a few birds, of course, Detective Inspector, but I'm not one for hunting.'

'Well, if I need to contact you?'

'Your daughter Claire knows the number if you lose the card,' Samantha added.

'Oh yes, you're one of her friends.' He sighed as he now remembered her, he had seen her fleetingly one day, picking up his daughter in some flash sports car. A wry smile crept across his lips. He loved his daughter very much. But she did mingle with some very strange types, it was best to leave alone. He had never understood women and he was too old to start trying now.

'Oh my word, my luggage. I nearly forgot!' Nicola exclaimed as she quickly put the mug down on the wagon's counter with a panicking glance to the train. The Detective Inspector smiled.

'Don't worry, missy.' He reassured her as he clicked his fingers. He looked over towards the platforms, where he noticed a tall, smartly turned-out porter with a sack barrow.

He was a black man, but at glance there didn't seem to be any white railway porters about, so, he clicked his fingers again and the porter turned, intrigued to know what was going on. As Detective Inspector Marriot beckoned him over, he called, 'Oi, You.'

The porter sighed heavily and reluctantly came over to them with his sack barrow.

'Would you bring these young ladies' luggage to the rank?' Detective Inspector Marriot commanded as both the women then handed the porter their luggage tickets and with a nod the porter started to make his way over to the platform.

'Thank you, Detective Inspector.' Nicola thanked him touching his sleeve briefly and as he smiled, his evening not totally ruined he thought, the constable by the police box, candlestick phone still in his hands, turned to the Detective Inspector and called out.

'Sir?'

Detective Inspector Marriot came over to him.

'We're connected now sir.' He handed Detective Inspector Marriot the phone.

*

The street was wide and lit only by a sparse spread of electric street lamps. Their bright white light reached out to the surrounding darkness, lighting a small disc around them over the kerb and into the road, but the buildings and the space between them remained as dark as the night sky.

On both sides of the street there were a number of dark shopfronts, selling things from ropes to slates and other industrial items while behind them factories rose like dark mountains casting a claustrophobic shadow over their street and making the night seem darker than it truly was. The stars were hidden by these manmade mountains, the backs of the factories, their tall chimneys reaching so high they seemed to hold the stars from falling from the sky.

On the corner of a crossroads, there was a blue pedestal police box, its blue light flashing.

A constable was standing by the box as a police sergeant came over to him, stopping him by his presence from opening it. The sergeant took out his own key and opened the box himself. As he lifted the phone, the flashing light went out.

'Sergeant Bull here!' He listened to his instructions before replying, 'Barlow's, that'll be Barlow and Sons. I know it, sir. Will do.'

He put the phone away and locked the box again. He turned to his constable and with an authoritative wave they started to walk up the road towards the factories.

5

The sunlight shone brightly against the mew's three-storey town houses. About three quarters of the way along the terrace sat a brightly polished, vibrant red one-door sports car with a long bench seat. Its soft canopy roof was folded back tight against its beetle-back boot and, with its matching swooping mudguards and running boards all as one reaching far over its large front wheels and long tall bonnet, she looked as fast as she looked sturdy.

On each wing at the front there was a small light but the headlights were mounted on a bar across the front of the radiator and, as was so common with modern sports cars, edging out just beneath them was the familiar double bow of the heavy coach springs. The spare wheel was fastened with the tool kit in a box on the running board next to the driver's position.

On its radiator embossed bright and proud was the inverted red triangle, shimmering as bright as the paintwork. The brand new Alvis 12/50 sports car in a prominent position out front was parked tight against the pavement before the small iron railing and the four steps that led up to the blue front door with its brass house number, 27, over its lion-head knocker.

There were other cars in the mews, but somehow none seemed to be so bright and none seemed to be as daring, each more sedate, more practical, not built for speed.

There were a small number of trees planted on the opposite side of the road and the sounds of birds could be heard twittering on the blossom budding branches.

Whistling his merry tune, if somewhat his own interpretation of an well-known arrangement, the milkman with his horse and cart left a bottle of milk on the top step of number 27, then continued along the road to the next house.

*

With a slip slap, Samantha's bare feet padded across the black-and-white tiled floor. In the middle of the room there was her large bath, its chrome taps to the centre on one side with the shower handset resting like a phone receiver in its cradle between them.

By the frosted glass window, stood the lavatory its pipe and cistern reaching up the wall, with the pull chain resting along the black painted window frame. At a right angle on the wall, just at a comfortable height when seated, hanging on a looping hook was a roll of Kleenex which the makers had suggested was good for removing cold cream, which it was, but even if it hadn't been their intention, Samantha had found it had a much better use, being as it was softer than the hard waxy sheets often sold for the purpose. On the opposite wall to the door there was a matching white sink with a medicine cabinet above it and another cabinet beside it in which were kept all the extra towels and other bathroom paraphernalia.

Next to the door and along the wall there was a radiator on which a towel was folded over. Samantha removed her plum dressing gown revealing her pale-pink silk pyjamas, and hung it up on the peg behind the door. She then crossed to the toilet, lifting the black Bakelite lid before ....

*

There was a brief knocking on the bedroom door before it opened and Albert entered. He was an average-looking man, with a quiet sense of dignity about him, in his black butler's suit with a yellow-and-black horizontally striped waistcoat, white gloves and black tie. He had short salt-and-pepper hair and was in his forties. Perched across the bridge of his nose he wore a pair of round, brown Bakelite spectacles.

He was carrying a silver tray upon which was a small teapot, a creamer, cup and saucer, teaspoon, but no sugar bowl and as he entered he glanced around the room, noticing that the bed was empty.

The room itself was a large rectangle, its length running from the one large centre window that looked out onto the mews.

The room was dominated by the double bed, the head end against the wall opposite the window and near to the door, with the headboard, foot board and springs all painted in a dark biscuit brown, without any inlays or decoration added, though around the top of the panels, both on the headboard and the footboard there were two parallel lines, moulded to follow the curve from one post to the other. There was an orange spread covering the blankets and the pillows and both the sheets were a shiny pink satin. Either side of the bed there were two bedside tables, both by the head end and on both there was a tall, slim chrome pedestal lamp with a wide red shade.

The one nearest the door stood there on its own but the far bedside table also had a copy of The Desert Moon Mystery by Kay Cleaver, resting by the brown barley twist cord that disappeared down the back of the table.

That side of the bed was also disturbed, the side she slept on, and so Albert proceeded to take the tray round the bed to that side, passing by the tub orange-and-brown armchair that faced the bed, crossing the small red rug between them that added a bright splash of colour on the tan carpet that covered every inch of the bedroom floor.

After placing the tray down so that it sat under the lamp, he felt along the cord until he found the switch and turned it off.

Behind him there were two paintings, one of a ballerina waiting in the wings of a stage waiting to go on, and another of a ballerina warming up, doing her stretches, as another in the background checked that her pumps were tied up properly. The pictures were hung either side of a large Armoires style wardrobe. Beside that, just to the side of the wardrobe door on the window side, there was a small chocolate-coloured clothes horse.

Albert crossed over to the golden tan curtains that hung behind the dressing table with its three-part fantail mirror. Scattered upon its surface was an assortment of silver-topped glass bottles, jars and atomisers, as well as a silver and mother-of-pearl backed hairbrush and a small matching hand mirror, Kleenex box and the great assortment of brushes and lipsticks any modern girl could need.

The picture rails, window frames and skirting boards were all the same brown as the bed and though there was a large disc-up shaded lamp in the middle of the cream ceiling, there were in regular intervals around the tan walls, a number of white clamshell uplights, none of which were lit. All the wall and ceiling lights were controlled by just two brass switches on a brass plate just inside the door.

On the other long wall, there were another two paintings, one of a ballerina on the stage, with the spotlight partially silhouetting her as she balanced herself on pointed toes, with one leg raised parallel to the stage.

The other was much the same, but the pose was different as if she was about to do a spin.

There was also, at an incline to the dressing table and the armchair, making a loose triangle, a full-length, free-standing mirror.

Above the headboard there was another painting of a ballerina taking her bow on the stage, flowers strewn around her as if they had been thrown by her admiring audience, while she relished their applause.

Albert slid both curtains back and used the rope tie to hold them open as he then peered out to the street below.

He could see the milkman was making his way back along the other side of the street, his horse following him, always a few houses behind as if on a silent cue, so that as he came down the steps, his basket full of empty bottles, the cart would be in front of him, and he could swap them over for some full bottles with their shiny red wax seals over their cardboard lids.

A wry smile crept across Albert's lips and he admired the chirpy happy attitude of the man. He felt the milkman must enjoy his work and seeing someone happy made him feel happy too.

Returning once again to his own duties, he crossed the room to the wardrobe, turned the key in the lock and opened out both of the central doors.

From it he took out a pale green dress, which he then placed delicately upon the second rail of the clothes horse, smoothing out any possible wrinkles, before taking from the drawers below a pair of similar coloured stockings which he draped over the top rail.

He closed up the wardrobe again, locking it before crossing over to the dressing table and from the second drawer down took out the light peach-coloured camisole and matching shorts and a suspender belt and placed these items on the horse's top rail.

He then carried the clothes horse over to set it down beside the armchair and, just as he did so, the door opened and as he looked over, greeting him to the accompanying sound of the toilet flushing echoing along the hallway, stood Samantha, pulling her gown tighter around her.

She closed the door.

'Morning, miss. Busy night?' he asked.

'Morning, Albert. And how,' she replied coming round the bed. She sat on the edge and began to pour her cup of tea.

'Will miss be partaking of breakfast this morning?' he asked, turning to her.

'Just toast and tea. Got to make an early start.'

She added a splash of milk.

'As you wish.'

'We'll have it in the lounge. I trust the paper has arrived?' she asked as she swung her feet up onto the bed and then picked up the cup and saucer.

'Ironed and waiting,' he replied.

She took a sip. It tasted so good and refreshing that she allowed herself a small, self-satisfied sigh.

'As always, you're so wonderful to me, Albert.'

'I try to be, Miss.'

'And our guest? Is she up and about?' Samantha asked, before taking another sip.

'Not yet, miss? Should I wake her?'

'No, no, she's had a hard night too. Best let her be.'

'Very good, miss.'

He bowed slightly and without any further word, he left her to enjoy her drink.

*

The hallway and stairs were starkly decorated. The walls were like the outside, white, with the banister rail and an occasional table that stood below a large mirror near the door being black. On the occasional table there was an ivory-white phone and a notepad with a pen beside it.

The carpet that ran up the centre of the stairs was the same shade of blue as the front door and behind the front door there was a blue mat, before the floor of black-and-white tiles, set in a harlequin pattern, which passed the coat stand next to the lounge door and turned towards the kitchen.

Albert made his way along the passageway to the front door, opened it and picked up the milk bottle. As he turned back, allowing the door to close softly behind him, he heard the faint sound of a floorboard creaking and on the upper landing, dressed in a long white nightdress and pulling her brown check gown around her, stood Nicola.

'Good morning,' she called down to him, feeling a little embarrassed, still disorientated by her new surroundings and unsure what to expect next.

'Good morning, miss.' He smiled sympathetically. 'Did you sleep well?'

Nicola nodded, not sure if she really did or whether because of the night's events she had just passed out with exhaustion.

'The milkman didn't wake you, did he?' he asked, indicating the bottle he held in his hand.

She smiled and shook her head adding, 'No, I slept like a log.'

'Good.' He was about to move on when he asked, 'Oh, I'm just about to make some breakfast. Miss Bishop is having toast with tea today if you would care for some? Or I could do you some scrambled eggs? Porridge? Now the milk's arrived.'

'Toast would be fine.'

'Tea or coffee?' he asked.

'Tea, please.' She paused for a moment, 'So...' and asked sounding as though she didn't wish to be prying. 'Miss Bishop lives alone then?'

'She's always been the sort of girl who likes to plough her own furrow.'

She smiled and nodded as she agreed.

'Come on down and I'll bring it to you in the lounge. That's where Miss Samantha is having it today.'

'Shouldn't I dress first?' she asked, gently tugging her robe around her more tightly, before checking that the bow in the cord was still holding it closed.

'No need for conventions here, miss.' He smiled. 'She's quite the bohemian and the kettle's already on.'

He then continued to the kitchen as Nicola paused for a moment, glancing back to her bedroom. Most of her clothes were still in her case and they were not as good as her green suit. In her mind she told herself, a green suit at breakfast wasn't the right thing to wear in polite London society.

Maybe Miss Bishop was being all so bohemian to just make her feel more comfortable, as she must have obviously suspected that after travelling all the way down from the North to find a job, Nicola wasn't going to have such an extensive up-to-date wardrobe as Miss Bishop would most certainly have.

But still it didn't feel right to her to be still in her bed clothes, especially for breakfast and at this time of day, whatever that time was. The clock in her bedroom she remembered wasn't wound, having stopped at four fifteen.

However, if Miss Bishop was dressed in her bedclothes, wouldn't it be rude not to do the same?

The decision was made, so she came down the stairs and crossed to the lounge.

6

Samantha, Nicola was pleased to see, was still dressed in her pyjamas, reading a newspaper, in one of the two cream and white tub armchairs, opposite the matching tub sofa.

She looked over her paper as Nicola entered and they both just smiled sweetly to one another, which made Samantha feel a little warm glow within herself, before she went back to her page, the glow still stretching out within her as she glanced up occasionally while Nicola looked around her to get a sense of the room.

The walls and ceiling were a warming peach colour and each was framed by a dark burnt-oak border, with the panels of the walls divided with the same dark brown into elongated rectangles. The floor was a bare highly polished herring bone, and the fireplace was black onyx, with a lamp standing either side like columns, each with a vibrant red shade   level with mantelpiece so that it looked as if they were hovering just over it.

There was an intricate chandelier in the centre of the ceiling and two pale-cream marble coffee tables in the centre of the room between the chairs. A mirror with black onyx inlaid borders hung on the chimney breast and below it, on the mantelpiece there was a bronze Chiparus statuette of an Egyptian belly dancer with her hands raised.

The curtains were peach and the cushions on all the seats were black-and-white striped and, though there were no paintings in the room, it still felt cosy.

In one of the back wall corners there was a small black pedestal table upon which there was a statuette of the Scarf Dancer also by Chiparus. In the other corner, immediately catching Nicola's eye, there was another table on which Samantha had a collection of photographs, mostly of herself during her time as an actress as well as a couple of her as a racing driver, but next to this, standing on the floor but taller by about four inches, was a large, dark, wooden box with a wire coming out the back of it.

Her bare feet padded over to the box and, lifting the lid up and away from her, she could see it was a gramophone player and she noticed in a rack under the gramophone there were over two dozen records.   More records she had ever seen in all her life and she was sure Samantha must have a copy of every record ever pressed. Removing one, her face lit up with delight as she noticed it was a recording by Tram, Bix and Eddie.

As she continued to look at the records, the lounge door opened and Albert entered with a large tray, on which were two racks of toast, a teapot, two cups with saucers, a creamer jug, a sugar bowl and two pots, one with jam and one with marmalade, and a small butter dish, all of which he placed on the coffee table nearest to the door.

'You have a very pretty place here,' Nicola sighed as she paused flipping through the records.

Samantha folded her paper back over on itself.

'Thank you. I like to be close to society,' she replied as Albert placed the two cups onto their saucers.

She then folded the paper over neatly and placed it into a black magazine rack that was down by her chair.

'Shall I pour?' he asked.

'No, Albert. I think we can manage now.' Samantha smiled.

'Very good, miss.' he replied with a small bowing nod.

'And an enormous collection of recordings?' Nicola was amazed. Carefully she took a disc out from its sleeve. Albert closed the double doors gently but firmly behind him.

'I mix a lot with society,' Samantha replied as she stood up and after adjusting her robe slightly, she leant over to pick up the teapot.

'Grooves well worn?' Nicola observed as she placed the disc upon the gramophone.

'I'm a very popular girl!' Samantha added as she started to pour the teas while Nicola looked at the box confused.

'Where's the winder?'

'It's electric.'

'Electric?'

'Yes, cost me £300, and 4 shillings for delivery, which I'm sure was overpriced. But well, it saves all that wrist ache.'

'£300! Neither of my brothers earns that in a year!'

'Just press the button.'

Nicola pressed the play button, the turntable began to spin. Then she set the stylus down gently upon the record and as the lid speaker crackled into life, the music began to softly fill the room. Swaying to the melody, she came over to where Samantha stood.

'Milk?'

'And sugar,' Nicola added.

'Yes, flower,' Samantha responded as she handed the cup and saucer to Nicola.

'No, sorry, I meant, I take one sugar too.'

As Nicola held her drink, Samantha picked up the sugar bowl and with her tongs she placed one sugar cube into her cup. Nicola stirred it in and, sat down on the sofa as Samantha picked up her own tea, added the milk and then sat on the sofa beside her.

'I have to thank you again for putting me up for the night,' Nicola added. 'I never knew people in London could be so friendly.'

'Well, I wasn't born here,' Samantha replied, before sipping her tea.

'Oh?'

'I'm from Whitstable originally, though my mother and I have moved around so much over the years, I suppose London's as home as anywhere these days.'

'Until yesterday, I'd lived on the Tyne all my life!' Nicola had to concede reluctantly as in Samantha's company she felt so inexperienced and so naïve about the world.

Samantha took a cigarette out of the silver box on the table and used the large matching lighter beside it. Then after taking a quick draw she added,

'You're welcome to stay a while.'

'Thank you.' Nicola drank some tea. 'But I should be looking for work today. If there was just an end to this beastly business.'

'I know!' Samantha took a sip and her cup clinked back into its saucer. 'What with factories, shops and banks closing every day, will there ever be an end to it? Millions on the dole! It's almost as grizzly as finding a skin on your porridge.'

'No, I meant that business last night on the train!?'

'Oh yes, that is a bit grizzly too!' Samantha agreed.

As they drank their tea there was a sudden loud knocking at the front door. She stubbed out her cigarette into a black onyx ashtray. She looked over to the clock on her mantelpiece.

'It's nearly eleven,' Samantha glanced quickly at her wrist watch as well, adding, 'who can be calling at this hour?'

Samantha held her cup with a thoughtful expression on her face as Nicola took another sip. She then put her cup down on the coffee table and placed a piece of toast onto a plate. Beside it she spooned some jam before carefully taking a slice off the butter and then spreading the butter and some of the jam onto a corner of her toast prior to eating that bit.

As she loaded some more butter and jam onto the next mouthful of toast, the lounge door opened and in came Albert.

'A Detective Inspector Warren, miss.' he announced as the detective followed him in.

'Miss Bishop, Miss White,' Warren began hastily. 'Sorry to disturb you both so early in the morning, but I've just come over from Barlow and Sons.'

'Thank you, Albert,' Samantha replied, placing her cup delicately upon the table.

'Miss.' He replied and left the room as Samantha turned to the Detective Inspector and asked,

'Barlow and Sons? Wasn't that the place where that man was murdered?'

'Yes, miss, it's only... .' He cleared his throat once. 'Well. Are you sure you saw the murder at Barlow and Sons?' He waited a moment for a reaction, but with none coming he continued, 'I only ask you this, miss, because, on examination of the site, it does appear that no murder has taken place!'

Confused and perplexed, Nicola turned to Samantha before she rounded on him.

'But I saw the man fall from the office window. Surely there must be some evidence of that!'

'You would think so, miss!' Detective Inspector Warren continued with a shrug. 'Maybe you just identified the wrong place? It was dark, could easily be done!? I was wondering if you would care to come over to Barlow's and see if you could identify the exact window for us?'

Nicola turned once more to Samantha, who nodded to her to reassure her and then, as Samantha stood, she pressed the round brass button next to the fireplace.

'That's okay, Inspector,' she told him. 'I'll run her down in my car and we'll see you there toot sweet?'

He nodded as Albert opened the door and, as Detective Inspector Warren left, Albert closed the door shut behind them.

'You believe me, don't you?' Nicola asked tentatively.

Samantha waited until she heard the front door close. She turned to Nicola and sat beside her.

'Of course I do.' She reassured her but Nicola wasn't so easily convinced.

7

Samantha's little Alvis roared down the wide industrial street before swinging left around the corner and along a narrower uneven cobbled road. As the spoked wheels bounced, rocking them both from side to side, Samantha and Nicola followed the road round and into the rear yard of the trackside factory.

They passed through the gap where the iron gates used to be to arrive in a wide, open yard. It was cobbled, with tufts of grass growing between the cobbles in places, and was littered with rubble and factory junk, stretching all over the area with a large amount of rubble, concentrated at the base of the railway embankment.

All around there were police officers combing the surrounds, kicking over empty tins of paint, large fragments of brick, broken window frame and sheets of tin, paper and sacking.

Two officers were working with dogs, others held long metal rods and were poking the overgrown brambles, piles of bricks and soil.

Over by their police car parked near the entrance to the yard, with the word Police in white on a plate over the front of the radiator, stood Sergeant Bull and Detective Inspector Warren watching their officers searching for clues.

Samantha pulled up next to them and as she pulled on the brake handle, she noticed Warren nod to her. The engine died. Then she and Nicola slipped out of the car and stood next to them.

'Miss Bishop.' Warren acknowledged her again, keeping his hands in his coat pockets as she took a cigarette from her handbag and lit it before replying in kind,

'Inspector.'

'Miss White. This is my sergeant, Bull.' Bull replied with a swift salute as Warren continued. 'Can you tell me at which window you saw the murder taking place?' he asked, looking up to the factory.

She looked up and was surprised to see that it was run-down with many of its larger rectangular windows smashed.

'There seems to be a lot of broken windows,' she conceded.

'But none large enough to throw a man out off,' Detective Inspector Warren added. Nicola glanced over them all but couldn't see the ones that had broken as she'd seen, the large hole she knew should be there.

'Don't know!' Samantha sighed. 'Have you tried?'

'The Metropolitan Police budget doesn't extend to throwing men out of windows, miss.' Detective Inspector Warren replied indignantly as Samantha sighed.

'Pity!'

Nicola squinted at the windows again, trying to compare what she had seen against what she could now see.

'It's hard to say,' she sighed.

'I know you're a northerner,' The Detective Inspector observed her with a little disdain, 'but try!'

'Only at night everything looks so totally different,' Nicola began. 'Probably because it was so dark?!! But I'm sure it was the centre office. That's where the light was coming from.'

Detective Inspector Warren showed them the way towards the entrance as he added, 'If you would be so kind.'

Then together the four of them started towards the building as Samantha tossed her cigarette away.

*

At the top of the stairs, they entered a large, wide, open room which was completely empty of anything industrial. In places the paint was peeling off the walls and in other areas there was smashed glass and wood where the dividing walls had been torn down and left where they'd fallen.

Paper, rubble and other waste littered the floor and the lighting above them was, mostly in place though, some of the plastic shades had been smashed and some of the bulbs inside were also gone.

Detective Inspector Warren's footsteps crunched over the broken rubble as he went further into the room and then turned back to the others, as they tentatively picked their way through the junk, both Samantha and Nicola trying to keep up with him. He smiled as he waited.

As Samantha stepped on a broken pane of glass, a large black beetle rushed out from under its frame and away from her and under a piece of broken brick. She looked around her. Even to the untrained eye, she thought, this place didn't seem to have been disturbed for such a long time.

'As you can see, miss,' Warren nodded to indicate the mess about him, 'this property has been empty now for weeks.'

Certainly an understatement she felt. This place must have been abandoned after the war. It was then that something began to puzzle her. For the first time since they'd arrived she felt things were too obvious, designed almost to discredit Nicola's account of what she'd seen.

'I fear one of the many that have succumbed to the problems from over the pond,' Detective Inspector Warren continued.

'I see,' Nicola replied, saddened by the mess around her.

'So, miss?' Warren asked. 'Are you still sure?'

'This could still have been the right place though, couldn't it Inspector?' Samantha asked, pointing up to the lighting above her. 'I mean, this place still has electric lamps hanging.'

Detective Inspector Warren nodded to Sergeant Bull who flicked all of a bank of light switches on a big board by the stairs but nothing came on.

'The local municipal electrical company switched the power off the moment that the factory became vacant.' Detective Inspector Warren explained before kicking a piece of door frame across the room away from them.

'I see.' Samantha began to look around the room. As the piece of wood was kicked, she noticed that there was a small cloud of dust. It was obviously the wrong place. Unless of course Nicola was wrong, but something in the back of her mind told her that Nicola was not the lying kind.

'I've lived in this area all my life,' Detective Inspector Warren continued, 'and now the old factories are making way for empty fields. What's the world coming to, eh?

When grass is more important than making rubber novelties?'

'Quite,' Samantha half-heartedly agreed.

'Well, as you can see, miss,' he kicked another piece of glass, before turning to both the women and continuing, 'this place can't be where you say you saw that murder taking place and as no body has yet been found, I have to ask you if you are sure you actually saw a murder in the first instance?'

'I am. Well. I'm sure I am.' Nicola was confused. She knew what she knew, but she also could easily tell that this wasn't the place. However if the Detective Inspector said this was the place then it had to be!

'Shall we?' Warren indicated the stairs, wanting them to leave, and reluctantly, feeling the disappointment of defeat, they followed Sergeant Bull back down the stairs.

8

They followed Sergeant Bull and Detective Inspector Warren to their cars and as they stood by the Alvis, Detective Inspector Warren turned to them, while Sergeant Bull went around to the front of the police car to turn the starting handle.

'Well, you just rest your pretty little heads and leave us to sort out this mess, miss. Miss Bishop.' He gave them a cocky salute.

They waited as he and Bull climbed into their police car and drove away.

'I was sure I saw something,' Nicola sighed feeling rather dejected.

'So am I,' Samantha replied turning to her. 'But maybe we're looking in the wrong place?'

'How do you mean?'

'I think this calls for a new perspective.'

*

The embankment was steep and both Nicola and Samantha had to take it easy, giving each other support as they slipped over the long uneven grass, but after a while they had reached the railway line. They carefully picked their way over the loose stone chippings that the tracks rested on until they had reached the Barlow and Sons sign.

'Well. There's the sign,' Samantha remarked as she looked back from the track to the ruined factory it seemed the sign belonged to. There was no doubting it. From where they were standing the empty factory had to be the right place.

Just then they were forced to move nearer to the edge as a train came trundling by and quickly the two women were engulfed in a cloud of smoke and steam. Samantha watched it pass and as the cloud faded away, she was surprised to see the train stop further along the track.

She looked hard down the line as Nicola coughed away the last of the sooty smoke. Samantha cried, 'The signal!'

Nicola turned at her blankly.

'We were stopped by a signal, correct?'

'I should jolly well say so,' Nicola replied as she recalled, 'They jolted me twice; I nearly lost all my travel-sickness pills! I have a very delicate stomach. I often get queasy if I can't see a horizon. Why, I was nearly sick every day taking the ferry to Gateshead all through the winter months.'

Samantha rested one of her white-cotton gloved hands on Nicola's stomach.

'Oh you poor thing.'

Such a soft and flat stomach Nicola had too and she didn't flinch an inch as Samantha rested her hand there.

There they stood, staring for a moment into each other's eyes. Just looking into her eyes filled Samantha with a warm infectious glow, which she thought was making her smile uncontrollably as she was beginning to feel all light and giddy. She wanted to move a little closer, too, but before she could say anything, there was a shrill whistle from behind her and she moved her hand away. Together they turned to look down the track to see, the semaphore arm had dropped.

'That's where we should be, down there, by the signal.' Samantha pointed as the train began to pull away slowly. They continued down the track, carefully picking their way over the loose chippings.

Standing by the signal, the pair looked over to another factory, this one busy, a company that was certainly still delivering from full order books. Smoke was bellowing from its four chimney stacks and from the windows, which were all in place, there was a hive of activity passing behind them.

Even the yard was full as men heaved heavy-looking, brown cardboard boxes up onto the back of a large flatbed lorry.

Samantha turned to Nicola.

'Well?' she asked. She could see Nicola trying to visualise what she was looking at compared to what she could remember of that night.

'It's not quite how I remember it, but ...' Nicola paused as she looked along the upper floor's windows, then she noticed it.

'You see the office windows?' She pointed and as Samantha's eyes focussed on the windows, she began to smile as it was plain to see and, for the first time since she'd fallen for those beautifully shapely gams, she had no doubt whatsoever that Nicola knew what she had seen from that railway-carriage toilet.

'I do,' Samantha grinned, 'the frame's another colour.'

'As if they've just been replaced!' Nicola added.

'Attagirl!' Samantha continued. 'And see, I told you, you were right. Come on. Let's go back to the car and then pay them a visit.'

'A visit?' Nicola asked, nervously. 'How can we just get in?'

Samantha smiled and rested a reassuring hand upon her shoulder. Small and delicate, soft to the touch, even though she could just feel the bone through her gloved hand. So fragile Nicola seemed and yet it was as if Samantha could feel a deeper strength rippling up from far down inside her, which made her feel all the more attracted to her.

'We'll pretend we're clients. They make rubber products correct?'

Nicola nodded, even though she didn't know what rubber products they actually made.

'Well, then, let's pretend we are in the market for some rubber goods. All we need now is a secretary.'

'I have good shorthand and can touch type!' Nicola reminded her and, as she gave her shoulder a reassuring rub, Samantha added, 'I'm sure you have, but we really need someone who can take notes and look as if they could write a letter.'

Nicola sighed patiently.

'I could do that.' But then a thought crossed her mind and she asked, 'Though, would just a secretary be out of the office on such a visit with her boss?'

Samantha paused to think for a moment.

'Wait a minute!' She exclaimed. 'Oh, this is so nifty. My chum Pinkie Stiff Fingers has a chum whose secretary he calls his Personal Assistant. If anyone asks, you're my P.A.'

9

The Alvis came to a sliding halt in the parking bay next to a silver-grey Rolls-Royce that was facing the factory wall.

As Nicola and Samantha climbed out, Samantha could see that there was a plaque on the wall just level with the Rolls' headlamps and in black letters on the white background it read 'Barlow MD'.

The factory was all dark red brick, five floors with rounded arches over each window, each of which was half as tall again as the height of an average man, made of small individual panes and held in a thin frame.

That was except for a row of six windows on the fourth floor.

These were more square and divided but without the arch. Like all the windows they were a set of smaller windows in a thin frame. Of these, one set, one from the end, was unlike the rest of the windows, which were painted white. These were unpainted, their newly installed wood only primed with a pink undercoat.

She looked back to the entrance and found that Nicola was standing by the door, holding it open for her, like the good little P.A. she was pretending to be and for the first time Samantha noticed what a cute little smile she had, the way the corner of her lips seemed to spring up to meet the sparkling of her narrowing eyes as if her whole face followed in the wake of her smile.

*

Samantha and Nicola were both led in by a young, pretty and slender girl in a light-blue blouse and dark-blue skirt.

She introduced them. 'Miss Bishop. Mr Barlow.'

'Thank you, Mary.' Mr Barlow replied, as he then offered a hand towards the two chairs before his desk.

Mary smiled uneasily and then as she turned to leave, he added, 'Could you arrange some tea for us, please, Mary?'

She nodded, 'Yes, Mr Barlow.' And as Mary closed the door behind them, Samantha took a glance around.

Barlow's office was large, the whole length of the six square windows and a quarter again divided each side of the end frames. The room itself was almost square, as it seemed almost as wide as it was long. The walls were all dark-stained oak panels, with a cream-coloured ceiling and the desk, side table and cabinet were all the same dark wood. Only the seating with red leather upholstery had any real colour, giving the room the feel of an old gentlemen's club.

Hung around the room were some industrial pictures of the factory in its earlier incarnation as well as a couple of landscapes which Samantha assumed were probably what this area of the country was supposed to have looked like before the Industrial Revolution had taken hold.

Barlow himself was sitting behind his desk. The inkwell and two pens protruding from it, though ornate in brass and black onyx, acted like a barrier between them as he sat almost swallowed up in his rather large and high winged-back chair.

He was a squat little man with thinning brown hair, which was beginning to turn grey. To show just how imaginative he was, he wore a brown pinstripe suit and a red tie, which almost matched the shades of brown and red in his office. He had a steely-eyed stare and seemed to be regarding them both intently, as if he wasn't sure what the proper procedure was for talking to a businesswoman.

Nicola took out her notebook and pen, having them already in her handbag in case she had been asked to prove her skills in an interview. She noticed this seemed to impress both Barlow and Samantha, and, to add to her apparent efficiency, she quickly flicked through the notebook, as if to find herself a clean page, before she waited, ready to take notes.

'You don't mind if my P.A. takes down our conversation?' Samantha asked politely.

'No, of course not.' he replied with an indignant shrug as if he had been expecting nothing less.

'Only she's like my right hand.' A devilish smile crept across her face, matched by a similar thought. She glanced over to Nicola adding, 'only prettier.' And was sure she saw her blush behind her notebook.

'Well, well, well, ladies.' He folded his fingers together so that they interlocked, resting his elbows on the arms of his chair. 'Did you find the tour of our plant informative?'

'Yes, thank you, Mr Barlow.' Samantha continued. 'You have a wide and extensive business here.'

'Yes, yes, yes, indeed. For nearly forty years now, the name Barlow has been associated with the manufacture of rubber invalid cushions, erasers for the ends of pencils, gloves for doctors and those of the veterinary calling, rubber balls and of course, our unmentionables.' He glowed with pride.

Samantha was confused.

'And just what are those unmentionables?' She asked.

'Oh, really, I can't say, well, not in polite company, you understand.'

She turned to Nicola who seemed to be as bemused as she was.

'Please, Mr Barlow, you can tell us?'

'I can't, Miss Bishop,' he protested, 'Really, that is to say, what I can say, I can only say because the product itself, I can say, I can't say, oh, well, not in such gracious company anyway, but what I can say, is that, let's say, shall we, that it's a late Friday night and a chap might, say, fancy a bit of something?' He cleared his throat, feeling a little uneasy and uncomfortable about continuing. 'We can't rightly say, it could be the other, that's to say, if he was to pop himself down to the chemist or if he, say, earlier in the day, had himself a haircut then what I can't say he might say, we'll say purchased the aforementioned, unmentionable, we'll say which will go a long way to seeing him right that night.'

They both looked blankly at each other as Mary entered bringing the teas, which she placed on the cabinet to the side opposite the windows. Then she turned to Nicola.

'One in mine, Miss Bishop has only milk.' Nicola instructed her.

Mary smiled and nodded and then set about pouring them their teas.

'You must be proud of your business? Build it up from scratch, did you?' Samantha asked.

'No, well, actually.' He paused watching Mary closely, as she placed the tea strainer over his cup, before answering. 'It was my father who built the company, but he died eight years ago.'

'Oh, I am sorry.'

'No need to be, he died as he wanted to.'

Samantha took her cup and Mary fetched Nicola hers.

'Running a successful business, you mean?' Samantha asked.

Nicola took her cup and held it in her lap as she balanced her notebook on her knee.

'No.' Barlow shook his head. 'In the arms of his twenty-one year old mistress.'

'I see.' Samantha sipped her tea.

'I took over then.' Barlow concluded.

'Which?' Samantha asked.

'The business, naturally.'

Samantha nodded as Mary placed Barlow's cup before him on the desk.

'So you are actually one of the Son's?' Samantha asked.

'Actually, the only one.' He corrected her before adding, 'My brother Donald unfortunately was killed in the war.'

'I'm so sorry to hear that,' she replied.

He watched the door close softly behind Mary as she left.

'Stroke of bad luck really,' he continued. 'He was run over by a tank whilst he was brewing up a cuppa in one of those shell craters. Made an awful mess of his kettle.'

'It would!'

'The horrors of war,' he agreed. 'When a chap can't even have a nice cup of tea without getting it.'

'The indignity of it.'

'Quite,' he agreed.

She let the silence pervade for a while, as she watched him mull over his family's loss for a moment before he continued.

'So I'm the last of the Barlows,' his rueful thoughts echoing his sullen mood, smothering the chink of light as he concluded, 'well, unless you include Donald's daughter of course.'

'Though if you do, you'd have to change the sign.' she reminded him.

'Yes.' He snapped back to his normal business-minded self. 'And money being a bit tight as it is at present. As you must know, Miss Bishop?'

She looked puzzled as she looked over to Nicola, who just returned a wistful smile.

'So you don't have any children of your own, Mr Barlow?' she asked, her attention turning back to him once more.

'No, no, no. My little filly prefers to lavish her allowance on fur coats and exotic trips to the Ritz Tea Rooms. The precious little thing that she is,' he sighed, adding, 'No, no, no, I can't see us ever having children.' He nodded past Samantha to the door. 'No, no, no, young Mary, she's our future. Mary, that's my secretary there, learning the trade from the bottom up. I'm a firm believer in the bottom up policy. Too many people neglect the bottom but you can have so much fun there, don't you think?'

'I certainly believe the bottom is a good place to have fun, yes.' Samantha replied.

'So I'm grooming her, so that someday, she can sit here, with me behind this desk, deliberating on whatever comes up.'

She looked around the room again.

'It is a nice office you have here.'

'Thank you.' Barlow smiled and watched her as her attention was drawn to his unpainted window frame.

'Unusual windows?' she commented.

'Eh?'

'The frames. Quite unusual?'

'Oh, oh, oh, yes. I see. No, no, no, you see, my office is being refurbished.'

'Thought you said budgets were tight?' she reminded him.

'They are,' he replied nervously, thinking on his feet, something which it was clear wasn't his strong point. 'Hence we've abolished the tea breaks, halved the lunchtime and extended the shift hours, but there's always enough money to refurbish my office. My office is in constant use from 9 to 5, so all the refurbishing work in here is done at night.'

'The factory is dark at night?'

'Not completely. Apart from the night watchman, we have half a dozen cleaning staff who work from 10pm when the last shift finishes though to four in the morning when the first shift starts.'

'Cleaning?' She asked.

'Cleaning out the extruder pipes that sort of thing.' He cleared his throat and then added, 'I mean, you can't have a blockage in your extruder now, can you?!'

'Quite!!' Samantha exclaimed, not too sure what an extruder was.

'So..., Miss Bishop. I'll have Mary send you our price list and I look forward to hearing from you in due course?' Samantha smiled as she sipped her tea.

10

Mary's office was much smaller, a desk in front of a number of filing cabinets and on the opposite side to the door there were more cabinets and Mary was squeezed into the small space between the desk and the cabinets.

Nicola was standing by the door to the corridor watching as Samantha was by the desk talking to Mary. She watched and admired the confidence and glamour she radiated. Samantha was an enigma for sure, all the manners and grace of one born wealthy and yet still with a common touch as if she was born poor. It was hard to know just what she was and those who tried to label her one way or another, Nicola felt, would feel uneasy around her as they would be sure to misjudge her.

The way she was with Mary now, she couldn't help but admire her.

Mary checked over the pages, checking the diary on her desk and after a quick scan down the page she turned shaking her head. It was with such ease she had persuaded Mary to do this task for her. You could feel that, given the chance, Samantha could even talk the King into washing her car for her, that was how confident and persuasive she could be.

Samantha thanked Mary before joining Nicola.

She smiled as if she knew something guilty and gently stroked Nicola twice on the arm before they both left the office as Mary watched them for a moment, bemused by it all.

*

As they approached the Alvis, Samantha suddenly stopped and Nicola paused too, bewildered as to what she was up to. She saw Samantha suddenly head for the railway embankment.

Nicola quickly followed, catching up with her just short of the rise to the railway line. Samantha stamped and began to look curiously at the ground by her feet.

'Are you okay?' Nicola asked, concerned as Samantha kicked the ground, but she didn't reply.

She kicked around again, exploring the ground. Then, she found some loose turf and slid it away with the side of her shoe, to reveal beneath a square patch, six inches wide.

Beaming brightly, she turned to the bewildered Nicola.

'As I suspected! The sign's been moved. Probably last night after we reported the murder to the police.'

'Yes. But who could have moved the sign?'

Samantha looked back up at the Barlow factory. From where she stood now, she could see the Barlow office clearly in front of her.

'Probably the same people who fixed that window late at night,' she replied adding, 'That's why they haven't painted it yet. There was no time. At any rate, even if we can't find the body yet, it gives us a clue and also might explain how they disposed of it.'

*

The Alvis roared down the wide main street, passing a horse-drawn cart, a trolley bus and two taxis.

A car in front cut across Samantha and much to her annoyance forced her to slow and change down to third gear. She hated it when she had to slow down. What was the point of having a fast car if you couldn't open her up? If it wasn't for the pedestrians and other traffic, driving in London would be a blast.

She pulled sharply upon the wheel to get around some car that was pulling out from the kerb and as she swung back to her lane again, Samantha was pleasantly surprised to feel the soft bump of Nicola as she slide gently into her.

The Alvis was a roomy car. Inside there was the red-leather bench seat that had a small space behind to store items such as a driving coat and a shelf in the dash to put one's driving gloves. The handbrake and the gear lever, with which she could select the four gears, were on her right, the handbrake being the one with the release lever you had to pull in first to be able to move it. At her feet were the pedals for the accelerator, the clutch and the brake pedal. It did have a crank, but also a self-starter, being very modern, and the steering wheel was large, almost as wide as Samantha, so easy to use.

The only door was on the passenger's side so it was always easy to get from car to pavement without risking standing on the dirty road, which was one of the attractions other than its speed that drew her to the Alvis. That and its collapsible roof, which, that day being nice and warm, was folded down behind her and could be quickly erected and fastened down in four minutes.

Normally she drove alone, but in the past with her oldest and close friend Porky and some squeeze, she had had the two of them on the bench seat and that was a bit rough. It restricted her arms when turning the wheel, which was hard enough after she had had a few down the club and, as Porky was never one to even try to learn to drive, getting them home was always down to her.

Nicola gently eased herself away as she asked, 'So where are we going now?'

'To the place where Barlow got his new windows from,' Samantha replied, reluctantly having to slow behind two horse-drawn carts as a trolley bus came from the other direction.

The gears clunked twice as she depressed the clutch and then shifted the gear stick to the centre, depressing the clutch again before pushing the stick forward one.

'And where's that? There must be hundreds of glaziers around London?' Nicola asked wondering if they were going to have to go to each in turn. But Samantha just smiled.

Wasn't she just so sweet?

11

They came to a gentle stop and the engine shuddered into silence. The Alvis rocked and was still.

Opposite them across the road, there was a set of large, double wooden gates, partly open, with the word Glazier painted in white across them both. There was a high wall either side but the shop itself was partly in view from the street, at the far end of the busy yard, past the many frames drying in the bright daylight, each propped against the long wooden sheds that led down to the office.

They could see that there were a number of men working, painting and moving the finished frames and they could also hear, though faintly, the sounds of hammering and a bandsaw cutting wood.

The street was in a rough-looking neighbourhood, with grim, dark-red brick back-to-back houses crammed together, jostling for space. None had a front or rear garden but there was a communal yard at the end of the street where every house kept their bins and hung out their washing.

The cramped pavements gave way to the narrow, pothole-strewn street in which the local boys and girls were playing, dressed untidily in their rough, ill-fitting clothes, with little dusty faces and beaten-up, scratched shoes on those who wore any.

Samantha pulled back on her handbrake until it locked in place. Then she glanced over to the glaziers and remarked casually, 'I just happen to know that in all of London, there is only one glaziers which carries out emergency window repairs late at night.'

'How?' Nicola was impressed. 'You've not been making a detailed study of tradesmen throughout the city? Knowing their practices and behaviours just in case such a crime was to manifest itself? Like some Sherlock Holmes?'

'No.' She turned back to Nicola, who in wide-eyed awe was staring back at her, and with a wicked grin replied, 'I asked Mary and she told me.'

Nicola sighed, feeling a little embarrassed. She then opened the car door slipped out. Samantha slid across and joined her.

*

The gaffer was a tall, wiry man with long, drooping jowls and a pale, tired, almost worn-out, look to his long, narrow face. Though clean-shaven, his face like his hands was as rough as the glasspaper used to smooth down the wood for painting and his white overalls were splattered with the many shades and hues of windows he'd repaired or replaced over the decades.

He stood behind his desk looking into a drawer of his filing cabinet. His desk was covered with paperwork, scattered and as untidy as the rest of his office. Standing patiently, with a little bit of fear that they might become contaminated by everything in this pigsty of an Aladdin's cave, Samantha and Nicola waited. Nicola, her book open, was taking notes.

The gaffer sucked back the air through his teeth as he slammed the drawer shut and started to move the papers on top of the cabinet from side to side as he muttered to himself.

'It's here somewhere, miss.' He paused to read a page, then as a faint smile cracked through his lips, he turned to them and continued, 'Yes, here it is! The invoice. One replacement office window to be completed in one night and one extruder waste tank to dispose of.'

Nicola wrote this in her notebook as Samantha asked.

'Tank?'

'Yes, miss. Mr Barlow was most insistent that we take the tank.' He wiped the end of his nose on his sleeve then asked, 'Why? Did we take the wrong one?'

'No, I don't think so. But there might have been something left inside.' He looked at her bemused as she asked, 'What did you do with it?'

'Well, it's out the back,' the gaffer replied, thumbing to the wall behind him as if they should have known. 'We don't take the scrap round 'til the weekend.'

Samantha smiled warmly. Her hunch was right. She started to feel that finally there might be some evidence to prove Nicola right. At last the police would have to take things seriously.

'May we take a look?'

'Sure?' The gaffer shrugged. 'And we're still okay for painting over the weekend?'

'Pardon?' Samantha quickly remembered the invention she'd used, pretending to be Barlow's secretary. 'Oh, yes. Carry on.'

The gaffer put the invoice down on his desk.

'Well then, miss.' He offered his open hand in the direction of the door behind them. 'You'd better follow me.' And as he came around the desk, they shuffled aside for him to pass, desperately trying to avoid everything in fear of stains being left on their clothes.

*

The glazier's rear yard was little more than a dumping ground for all the waste materials, glass, wood, rope and old tools thrown and left wherever a space could be found.

Against some broken window frames, was the large extruder tank. It was lying on its side. There was a hole near the top of it, half way up its side and high off the ground. Samantha and Nicola carefully picked their way between the fragments of broken wood and glass, following the gaffer as he just sauntered through.

'That's the tank.' He pointed to it as Nicola and Samantha sighed as one, having worked that out for themselves.

'Oh, look.' Nicola pointed as she noticed it. 'There's a hole in the top!'

'Do you have some steps?' Samantha asked.

The gaffer clicked his fingers towards a nearby worker, who disappeared momentarily behind the building and returned with a large 'A' frame set of steps, which like everything, it seemed, was covered in multi-coloured splatters of paint. He placed the steps next to the tank and, after he and the gaffer had steadied them, Samantha gingerly made her way up.

At the top there was a flat step like a platform, which she stood on. With an outstretched hand, she held onto the side of the tank, steadying herself as she swayed slightly.

Samantha took a calming breath and turned on the balls of her feet so she was able to peer into the darkness of the hole. She was suddenly almost overwhelmed by the strong stench of stale rubber and its overpowering aroma made her want to wretch. She momentarily looked away, took a deep breath as she told herself not to wretch and held her breath so she wouldn't, as she knew everyone around her was watching. Carefully as she held on to the edge of the hole with both hands, she leant over and looked in.

She shuddered slightly. Although expected, it was still a shock to see.

'Oh dear,' she called back as she turned to look down to the others, 'Not quite what I think Mr Barlow was hoping we'd find. I say, gaffer. You'll need to call the police. Ask for a Detective Inspector Warren, Scotland Yard.'

12

Samantha put the cup on the saucer and then placed them back on the table beside her. She picked up again her newspaper she had rested on the sofa beside her and went back to reading an interesting article.

The room was silent, but for the gentle tick of the clock on her mantelpiece, and she was able to be quiet with her thoughts at last.

It had been a few hours now since they'd left the glaziers. She had changed and placed her dirty clothes in the linen basket. The rubber residue she hoped would eventually wash off and now, as a cigarette burned in the chrome ashtray on a tall slim pedestal next to her, she was trying to put aside what she'd seen by reading how there was concern over the grain harvests in Kansas as apparently, if they had a bad harvest again, it could affect the world's banks in some way she didn't really understand or care for.

As she read on, her train of thought was broken momentarily by the sound of a knock at the front door.

Carefully, she folded the paper to keep her place, lying it beside her again before picking up her tea and taking a sip.

There was another knock at the front door so, holding her tea, she stood, replacing the cup on the saucer and then straightening her jacket so it wouldn't look too rumpled.

She waited by the mantelpiece and turned to the lounge door when she heard Albert open front door and say, 'Good afternoon, Inspector. Please come this way.'

The lounge door opened and Albert stepped aside to reveal Detective Inspector Warren, who was looking a little flustered as he removed his hat and entered.

'Good afternoon, Inspector. I assume you have news for me about the man we found in the extruder tank,' she asked.

'Indeed I do, miss.' Detective Inspector Warren immediately replied as Albert left them, closing the door.

He fidgeted with the brim of his hat for a moment but before Warren could continue, the door was flung open as, dressed only in her robe and with her head in a towel, Nicola entered, all excited.

'I must say, Sam, that contraption of yours is amazing!! Who would have thought being sprinkled on from a great height would have been so much fun?'

Warren turned to Samantha with an enquiring yet surprised smirk creeping across his face and already Samantha was beginning to feel a little embarrassed herself. Nicola removed her towel from her eyes and seeing the Inspector, she blushed.

'Oh, I beg your pardon. I didn't know we had company.'

'That's quite alright.' Warren shrugged.

'Why don't you go and get dressed, Nicky? I'll entertain the Inspector,' Samantha suggested.

Feeling so embarrassed that her cheeks were beginning to blush, Nicola left them, almost as quickly as she had arrived, closing the door firmly behind her.

Samantha sat in her armchair near the fireplace.

'I have a shower installed, in the bath' she began to explain, feeling the need to do so, just in case the Inspector was beginning to think she ran a house of ill repute. 'Well, sometimes one doesn't have the time for a soak.'

She sipped her tea.

'Quite!' He raised his eyebrows and then crossed to the mantelpiece. She could tell that there seemed to be something troubling him.

'You were going to tell me a bit about the man?' She reminded him as he leant against the mantelpiece with one hand as if he would fall over if he didn't. He had been up all night and the lack of sleep was beginning to get to him.

'There's not much to tell really. We haven't been able to identify him, as there was no wallet, nothing with his name or address on.'

'Wasn't he wearing a ring?' she asked.

When she had first glanced in, after her initial shock at seeing the grotesquely twisted expression on the poor dead man's face, she had noticed something glittering on the little finger of his right hand. Something golden, it had to be a ring.

'I'm sure I saw it on his finger inside the tank.'

'He was. Strangely enough, I have it on me.' Warren fumbled inside his coat pocket until at last he found it and handed the small golden ring to her.

Samantha placed her tea on the table. The ring rested in the palm of her hand and she examined it more carefully as the Inspector continued.

'Nothing remarkable about it.' He shrugged. 'It's just a normal gold ring.'

'With a pattern on the face,' she remarked, holding it up so he could see.

He just shrugged and asked, 'Which means...? What?' She looked at it again, three letters interlaced with each other, R.F.C.

'I don't know? But I think I know a man who might?!' She clutched it in her hand and then slipped it into her jacket pocket, continuing. 'Do you mind if I take it with me, Inspector?'

He shrugged as he had already got all he could from it.

'Provided I can have it back.' He wiped some imaginary dust away from the edge of the mantelpiece as he tried not to notice the naked thigh of the Egyptian dancer. 'I don't see why not? At this moment we're treating him as a vagrant, a missing person.'

'Not as our murder victim?'

'Murder, miss?'

'Don't you think this could be the man, Nicky,' she paused to correct herself not wishing to sound as if they were too familiar, 'I mean, Miss White, thought she saw from the train carriage?'

'Just because his body was found in the extruder tank doesn't mean he was murdered at the Barlow factory!' The Inspector pointed out before he continued. 'After all, none of the workmen at the factory are reported missing.'

'Maybe he didn't work for Barlow?'

'True, miss,' he reluctantly conceded.

'His clothes were too good to be a worker's,' she added. She'd noticed how bright the lining of the jacket had seemed in the half-light that had reached in behind her and she knew enough about fine tailoring and invisible stitching to know no one on the sort of wages paid at Barlow's or even at the glaziers would have had something so well made or so well fitting as the dead man had had.

Well-fitting clothes, a gold ring and clean-shaven, he was beginning to seem less like a vagrant or missing person with every passing second the more she thought about it. It seemed to her that even the Inspector must have noticed this too, but she couldn't understand why he wasn't acting upon these facts.

'But it's just as likely that he was a vagrant. Maybe they prove he was once a very popular man.' The Inspector defended himself, sensing that look on her face could lead to trouble if he didn't convince her now that the case was as good as closed. 'But who's to say?' he added. 'His fortunes could have been lost in the present financial difficulties?'

'True, but most unlikely. Some factories may have closed but the deflation's not wiped out our ability to trade!' she snapped back.

'True!?' He thought quickly for another explanation. 'Okay, maybe he was given the clothes.'

'Fine.' She could see that one as a possibility, but the clean-shaven face still didn't seem like a face worn by the rigours of the road, open to the elements and burnt by the sun.

In her mind there was this nagging doubt. She was sure this man's last few years at least had been spent in the comfort of a home and he'd worked inside, maybe an office or somewhere like that.

'Maybe he was cold,' the Inspector continued, still feeling that he needed to explain all the possibilities to her. 'It was a very cold night, miss. Maybe he took it upon himself to climb into the extruder tank, looking to keep warm and when the workmen took the tank away that night, they unintentionally, shook him so violently that they accidentally broke his neck and that's why he was still there in the afternoon when you found him, miss.'

'Have you tried the bespoke tailor shops?'

'We went to Sandler and Sons and no one there remembers him.'

'Why them specifically?' she asked.

'Where the clothes were made,' Warren conceded with a shrug, 'seemed a logical choice!'

'I see.'

'But nothing came of it,' he added. 'That's why I think he could have been given the suit. I tell you, Miss Bishop, he's nothing more than a vagrant.'

'I see.'

'I've seen it many times before,' he insisted.

'Have you?'

'Yes, of course.' He cleared his throat. 'They were probably donated to a charity shop. There's a lot of vagrants on the streets these days. Let's just face the facts, Miss Bishop. This poor unfortunate climbed into the tank at the back of the glaziers and was overcome by the fumes from the rubber residue and succumbed to asphyxiation.' That was it. He was sure that would do and concluded, 'Well at least, that's what my report's going to say. Now, you two young fillies carry on enjoying yourselves and leave the real detective work to us chaps, okay?'

Samantha smiled sweetly as she watched Warren leave, convinced in her mind at least that she was dealing with a murder and that she was going to prove it.

13

As Samantha drove her Alvis along the busy wide road, she waved her right arm up and down a couple of times to let the traffic behind her know she was slowing. Then she turned in toward the pavement, coming to rest a few yards further on.

Across the road, as they swivelled round on the seat, they could see the shop front of Sandler and Sons. It had two grand windows either side of the entrance door, which was set back a few feet so not to be on the pavement itself.

The suit jackets and hats on display showed both the quality and the styles offered, which to Samantha's sharp sartorial eye were a bit old-fashioned, certainly a little last season at least.

Samantha and Nicola turned to face the front again.

'Are you sure Sandler and Sons will be able to help us?'

'Yes,' Samantha replied adding reluctantly. 'But, this time we're going to have to be a bit subtle and I'm going to have to do this one. Alone.'

She waited as Nicola opened the car door and stepped out before she slid across and followed.

Nicola climbed back into the car and watched a little apprehensively while Samantha picked her way through the traffic, around the back of a horse and cart and over to Sandler and Sons.

As she entered the shop, the little bell tinkled above her head and she was greeted with the faint smell of cedar wood, leather, musk and tweed, all the honest smells of the countryside as she remembered it from her time in Scotland. She could see from the selection of walking sticks in a drum near the door that the great outdoors was one of their top lines.

The door closed itself behind Samantha. She looked around the room, a large open space, against the walls racks and drawers, stretching from floor to halfway to the ceiling and in which were socks, ties, vests, jumpers, shirts and underwear, each labelled above each drawer's half-dome handles.

On top of these there was a great selection of boxes of various sizes, except on the back wall, where there was shelf upon shelf of fabrics.

Running around the room like a glass horseshoe in front of the shelves were the counters, broken at the corners of the room so that they were kept in their appropriate sections, country, city, leisure and sport, and in these counters on display were the smaller items, the cufflinks, handkerchiefs, tiepins and other such gentlemanly apparel no smartly dressed gentleman should be without.

There were several staff, six she thought at first glance, all men, two of whom also had draper's tapes adorning their shoulders as if they were wearing a scarf, or more like a badge of office like the City's Mayor.

She felt a little self-conscious as if she was standing in her underwear and being examined when the shop staff looked across to her. It almost seemed she was going to catch fire from the embarrassment and she felt she should just turn and run away screaming as it appeared to her none of them had ever seen a woman before.

But getting control over her desire to run back to the safety of her Alvis, she took a deep steadying breath and headed over to the nearest counter, where stood an elderly, kindly looking, somewhat portly gentleman with thinning grey hair and silver-rimmed glasses, which he balanced on the end of his nose.

He smiled warmly as she came over to him and tilting his head slightly towards her he asked politely, 'How may I help you, madam?' He indicated the display in the case in front of him. 'Looking for a tie or something for your father or husband?'

She was still feeling nervous, the butterflies were flapping madly and it was all she could do not to shake, but at the same time she had to go on as this fear seemed to be exhilarating as well.

'It's alright. I'm not actually here to purchase anything for a gentleman.'

He looked aghast before he replied, in a patronising yet still pleasant way.

'Well, I'm sorry, miss, but we don't actually sell women's clothes here. We are only a gentleman's outfitters and we manufacture suits.'

'That's alright. I'm not looking for a suit either,' she replied.

'Then how can we be of service?' he asked, somewhat bemused.

Samantha took a deep breath. She wasn't so nervous now. She knew she had his attention and his curiosity and this gave her the confidence she needed.

She began to come across all coy and sheepish and then for a moment, it looked to him as if she was going to cry, something which he hoped she wouldn't because that was one thing he didn't know how to deal with, women crying. After all, that's why he worked in men's outfitting.

'Well, it is a little delicate,' she whispered to him and she leant a little closer to him, beckoning him to come a little closer to her.

'We're used to handling delicate matters here, miss.'

'Well.' Samantha glanced nervously into the shop to make sure no one else could overhear them. 'I'm trying to find this man. The sweetest, most loving man one could ever hope to meet.' She checked again no one else was listening. 'We met a couple of months ago at a party and we've been walking out ever since. The problem is... .' She took a deep breath and paused as if she was about to cry. He offered her his top-pocket handkerchief, but she smiled warmly as she gently waved his offer away, seeming to regain her composure. 'He's married.'

He drew a sharp intake of breath quickly as the shock hit him. The morals of the young were much more lax than in his day. No one in his day would have done such a thing, or at least if they had, they wouldn't have confided it to a stranger, and if they had, only if drunk and most certainly not like here and now in a working environment. But he was determined not to pass judgement on her, no matter how loose she was, or this cad for that matter, and after he gave her a weak little smile of reassurance, Samantha continued, 'Which wasn't a problem for me, I mean. He's so sweet and good-natured with it, and so generous.'

'He sounds it!'

'The problem is,' she paused as if the words were stuck in the back of her throat, 'and this is the nub, as to my shame, I must find him soon. You see, after all our dalliances, we now have a little issue.'

She glanced down towards her belly and the elderly staff member was again overcome with shock.

'I see.' And he was sure his brow was sweating. He was beginning to feel a little hot and light-headed, such goings-on were quite the scandal in a gentlemen's outfitters, as he asked, 'Do you know his name, miss?' And he hoped it wasn't one of his members of staff.

'Oh, well.' Samantha stammered. 'You'll feel we've been so terribly English. We never got around to properly introducing ourselves.'

'I see!'

'However, I do know he bought his clothes from here.' She emphasised this by pointing to the floor of his shop and he was a little relieved that it wasn't one of his staff.

'Yes, miss. We are renowned for having an intimate relationship with our clients and I would love to help, but we see so many gentlemen, it's hard to remember who's who.'

'That's fine, I understand. That's why the last time we were together, I fingered his ring.'

'We don't have that intimate a relationship with our gentlemen, miss!' he replied almost outraged but relaxed as from her handbag she took out the gold ring to show him.

'As you can see, it's ever so distinctive,' she remarked as he took it and had a good look at the design on its face.

'It most certainly is.' He handed it back to her and she placed it back inside her handbag. 'This is a ring that denotes that your gentleman friend was a member of the Royal Flying Corps. It's the Royal Flying Corps motif, from the war, before they became The Royal Air Force.'

Samantha was suitably impressed, though she'd seen many airmen during the war, she had been too young to notice things like rings and emblems. She had spent most of the war, both struggling to eat and living with the constant fear that the Germans would overrun Paris, where her mother had sent her to private school before going on

79

to work in Germany and had found herself trapped there when war had broken out, neither able to get to her mother or back to Britain.

The only thing she really remembered or cared to remember of that time was the French she'd learnt after four years. She could speak it almost as well as any native.

The assistant thought for a moment as he tried to put a face to the ring.

'Do you know! I think I do know who this man is!'

She followed him as he crossed the room to a desk at the back of the shop.

'You recognize the ring? I'm ever so glad.'

'It's a very distinctive ring, miss.' He opened a drawer and took from it a large, heavy-looking ledger. 'If I remember rightly. He didn't actually fly those kites during the war. He was a photographer. He took the pictures of the movement of the frontline.'

'They moved the frontline?' Samantha was surprised.

'Well, I'm not sure about that, but I do believe he owns a shop in town. One moment, I'll just check his details.'

He flipped through the pages of his sales ledger and after a few dozen pages he paused, turned back a couple, and tapped the name in the book.

'Yes, Malcolm Cooke,' he announced proudly. 'Has a shop along the Tottenham Court Road.'

'Thank you.' Samantha shook his hand. 'You've been most helpful.'

14

The tall, thick foliage of the yew tree swayed gently in the soft breeze, bending in time to the rhythm of the delightfully varied chorus of the birds.

Surrounded by all this, adrift in a sea of green with stone islands, stood the tall-towered, blue-flint church, its large and heavy oak doors open revealing the stone seats in the porch where, squinting slightly into the low sunlight, the vicar stood with a very young couple, both dressed in their 'Sunday' best clothes.

Over at the far side, behind all the gravestones, there was a loud squeaking noise and the vicar could see that the sexton was pushing the wooden wheelbarrow near the surrounding wall, the barrow filled to almost overflowing with pulled-up weeds, dead flowers and clumps of moss.

The vicar smiled to himself reassured. It was always a joy to see people busy on such a lovely day, reaffirming within his mind that God was great after all.

His mind wandered away from the sexton and returned to the young couple. With a heavy sigh, he asked, 'Are you sure you want to call your daughter Courtney, Mr and Mrs Fish?'

*

As he opened the low, wooden lychgate, Barlow glanced along the gravel walkway to see the vicar with the young couple and for a moment he hesitated. He didn't want to have to come back. His time was precious but he could see the vicar was busy. He was about to turn and go, when the vicar shook hands with them both and, as the young couple came walking down the path towards him, he straightened and with a renewed confidence he continued purposefully along the path.

Seeing Barlow, his old familiar friend, the vicar smiled and with a warm, open gesture he welcomed him.

'Mr Barlow! Twice in one week. To what do I owe this pleasure?'

'Are you busy, Vic?' Barlow asked, glancing around him and noticing that the sexton was heading back down the graveyard, his barrow left behind, and was probably off to have a tea break.

'Is there something troubling you, my son?' Barlow nodded. 'Business?' Barlow shook his head and the vicar knew this was serious.

They had known each other since the war. He had been their regimental chaplain and Barlow, the young fresh-faced captain leading his men over the top. It was that horror, the slaughter of the trenches and the guilt of surviving all that, which had eroded Barlow's confidence.

Then he had inherited the family business and

whenever he was in need of spiritual guidance, he had turned to his old friend and regimental chaplain. And he in turn was always there to help his friend. 'Then come this way!' The vicar replied pointing his way towards the lychgate.

*

The vicar led him down a small side road next to the church wall which led to the vicarage.

In the neatly kept and cosy lounge the two men sat opposite each other, either side of the fireplace in a pair of bright-red, high-back armchairs, with a white embroidered cover over the ends of the chairs' arms and a similar antimacassar over the back of the headrest.

The room was small, with a bookcase in one corner and dark oak occasional tables next to each armchair, as well as a round coffee table next to the matching sofa that was deeper in the room.

Near to the door there was a bureau where Barlow suspected the vicar wrote his sermons and there was a large lamp in the opposite corner and on the long wall there was a painting of a scene of some mountain range in Scotland between the crucifix and a portrait of Christ.

The curtains were like the wall, green in colour, but whereas the walls were light, these were a much darker hue, with an off-white lining to make them thick and keep the room warm in winter.

'So what seems to be the trouble?' the vicar asked as he tugged on a rope bell-pull that rested along the chimney breast.

'I really need some advice,' Barlow began, as a young woman in a service apron appeared in the doorway.

'Tea for two, please, Sally?' With a small curtsy she left them and Barlow noticed how the vicar studied her bottom as she walked away.

The vicar turned back to him.

'I do so enjoy tea in the afternoon, don't you?'

'Yes.' Barlow replied, suspecting he knew why. But he had to steer the conversation back to his own problems. 'Though I'm not sure I can really enjoy any toasted muffins at this time!'

'You really do have a problem!'

'I really do!' Barlow agreed.

'As bad as last time?'

'Worse.' Barlow admitted, crossing his legs and fidgeting nervously as he continued. 'And I was hoping that with the Lord's guidance you may be able to help?'

'Just what is the problem?' the vicar asked, listening carefully, drawing up his fingers as if to pray and bringing them to touch his lips.

The young girl returned with a tray which she placed on the coffee table. On the tray there were two china cups with saucers and a teapot for two people as well as a cake stand on which were some cakes, muffins and crumpets and plates with knives, cake forks and a milk jug, a sugar bowl with tongs and a strainer.

'There have been,' Barlow continued thoughtfully, 'some people I've had to do business with who have turned out to be less than desirable.'

'Thank you Sally. That will be all.'

She curtsied slightly and then left them to it as the vicar rose from his chair and poured the two teas.

'Well, the Bible told us, to cast those fellows out.'

The vicar handed a cup to Barlow and then placed a muffin on a plate. He took his cup and the muffin with him and sat down again as Barlow replied.

'I've done that, but it's caused another problem, well, two in fact.'

'Are these men of business too?'

'No, they're women.'

'Then what's your worry?' The vicar shrugged as he took a sip of his tea.

'But they're nosy women!' Barlow exclaimed. 'The sort that are likely to tell all they know about me!'

The vicar gently placed his cup back upon its saucer.

'Gossips?' he asked.

'Of the worst kind!'

'And you wish to seek the Bible's guidance?'

'Please?' Barlow implored his friend.

The vicar nodded as he understood. He sipped his tea and then carefully placed his cup back on the saucer before putting it down on the occasional table next to him.

He picked up his plate, holding the butter-drenched muffin, looking at it as if in reverence for its simple wholesomeness. He then took a quick bite before returning it to his plate and placing that by his tea.

He stood and, with a positive, determined stride, crossed over to his table next to the bureau and, as he finished chewing, he picked up the Bible that lay closed on it.

'To discover the truth, we must let the Bible speak to us,' the vicar continued. 'Ask the Lord for his guidance and you will find that where the page opens, the answer to your prayers will be there.'

Holding the book by its spine in one hand, he let the book fall open and as the pages stopped flicking and the book came to rest before him, he put his finger down firmly on a passage, without studying or without aiming at anything in particular.

'Well? Has it worked?' Barlow asked.

'This might help?' He cleared his throat and read aloud. 'Romans 1, chapters 29 to 32. They were filled with all manner of unrighteousness, evil, covetousness, malice. They are full of envy, murder, strife, deceit, maliciousness. They are gossips, slanderers, haters of God, insolent, haughty, boastful, inventors of evil, disobedient to parents,

85

foolish, faithless, heartless, ruthless. Though they know God's righteous decree that those who practice such things deserve to die, they not only do them but give approval to those who practice them.'

Barlow smiled contentedly to himself.

'You know. I feel better already.' And he took a long refreshing swig of his tea.

15

There was the ghostly glow from the pale, white electric streetlights shining through their plate-glass prisons, casting a feeble circle of light around their posts, not strong enough to quite touch the circle of the next one. Behind them stood the shops that lined either side of the road.

All was still. Not a soul walked along the pavement. The only visible signs that anyone had ever been there were the windblown sheets of paper, old brown bags, the lost pages from a newspaper and the leaflets that advertised the latest must-have at one or more of the shops, discarded by the passing trade and not yet swept away as the night crawled ever closer to the small hours.

The breeze had died, the air was still, silence.

Suddenly the throbbing roar of a powerful engine shattered this peace. Two large headlamps appeared, their yellowish-white beams stretching out to illuminate all before them, like two hungry eyes devouring all that they could see with their brilliant light.

The Alvis, its little canvas roof drawn up, glided along the road, before coming to a gentle stop, its drum brakes squealing their protest as the engine purred, outside a store two up from Cooke's Photographic Shop.

Quickly the engine died and almost instantly the headlights went out.

The door swung open and out stepped Nicola. She waited a yard or so away nearer to the shops as Samantha slipped out, closing the car door behind her.

She was about to lead the way when she noticed that the store they were in front of was having a sale on their coats and the one in the window with the white fur-trimmed collar seemed just the bee's knees.

Nicola tapped her on the elbow, pointing to Cooke's shop, reminding her why they were there. Samantha made a mental note that this store was worth coming back to as she just had to have that coat.

Together they walked along the road until they were in front of the camera shop and as she looked up at the number in the awning sign above the window, she reassured herself that they were at the right place. Nicola watched as Samantha went back to the car and took from the boot her little black bullseye lamp, which she switched on before closing and turning the handle a quarter turn to lock the boot again.

She turned the lamp off again then joined Nicola by the shop front then as she looked up to the flat.

'The flat above looks dark. Nobody's in.'

'Do you think there is a back way in?' Nicola nervously asked.

Samantha looked along the shopfronts, spying an alley not too far away from them at the other side of Cooke's shop. 'Shall we have a look?'

It was dark and narrow, made to feel all the more so by the high walls of the two shops with their two extra floors above them.

With none of the street light penetrating further down than a few feet in they had to use the bullseye to see their way.

This drive to electricity was never going to catch on, Samantha thought, as their light was never as strong as gas. The small round light from the bullseye shone before them enabling them to see the inward camber and the dry channel in the centre of the alley, the litter and mud. Carefully, the two of them picked their way along until they came to a tall wooden gate, inside a wooden frame, both of which were rounded, in an arch- and dome-like symmetry.

She caught sight of the latch in her bullseye and depressed it. It was stiff, but with one sharp push, the gate slipped back, creaking slightly on its rusted hinges and scraping the cobbles in the yard as it had sagged from years of neglect.

The two women tentatively entered.

The yard was small and walled all around a cobbled area with a slope to the centre at which there was a sunken drain. Facing them as they entered was the small toilet, its own latched wooden door firmly shut, darkness within, and to their right, facing back towards the road was the one window and back door to the shop.

Finding the door handle, Samantha tried it.

'It's locked.' She shone the light into the keyhole as she peered into it. 'And the keys in the hole!'

'I'll open it for you.' Nicola whispered and as Samantha stepped back Nicola suddenly threw a cobblestone through one of the small glass panes in the door, just above the handle.

The crash of splintering glass seemed to be so loud she was sure they would have heard them as far away as Faversham, but after a moment's wait, Samantha looked up to the flat above, but there was no light or movement and she began to relax and took a deep calming breath.

Her heart was racing wildly. It was she knew a heady mix of excitement and fear, the best combination she thought, as it seemed to fill her with a joy of overwhelming excitement but at the same time, the slightest fright and she was sure she would drop down stone dead.

She let the light from the bullseye shine through the window next to the broken one as she leant through and with one twist of the key opened the door.

'Keep quiet inside, okay?' she whispered to Nicola. 'We don't want to draw attention to ourselves.'

Nicola nodded as they entered.

They were in a small kitchen with another door opposite them and without pausing for long they passed through and into the main shop.

They entered behind the horseshoe counter that ran along the back and side walls of the shop, facing out to the wide window and narrow front door.

The room was in darkness but for the ghostly light of the streetlights. All the displays and goods that seemed to cover every inch of counter space and cluttered the window were in silhouette.

The beam of the bullseye reached out across the counter, illuminating in its small circle the cameras under the glass top and the packets of films, lens cleaners and other paraphernalia relating to how to take the perfect photograph.

Together they began to weave their way through the store, passing through the counter to the customer floor, where there were a couple of column display cabinets full of cameras on a number of plinths of different heights. The lamp's beam, flicked from side to side as Samantha gazed more upon the stock than watching where she was going.

'Nice stock, a few Box Brownies, Kodak, No.2

Folding Autographic Brownie camera. An Ica, Ensign, KVP 127 roll folding camera.'

Nicola was impressed by her knowledge. It was clear Samantha was a bit of an expert but she felt she was beginning to forget why they were there.

'Didn't realise we were shopping,' she said nervously as her eyes darted side to side looking for the danger she knew was lurking in the shadows.

'We're not!' Samantha agreed.

'So what are we looking for?'

'His desk,' Samantha replied. 'He should have a ledger, some transaction of sales, something which might suggest....' Then something caught her eye as she held the light on it a little longer. She cooed, 'Ooow, if you will!'

Nicola looked but she didn't know what she was looking at. It was just a long flat Bakelite box as far as she could tell with a little lens sticking out the top.

'A Houghton, Ensign Focal Plane roll film 120 single lens reflex camera.' Samantha announced as if she'd just discovered the Holy Grail and moved closer to it to look at it more precisely. ' It gives you the ability to view the image as the film sees it. It has a self retracting mirror, so it's so easy to transport, and it's so light I've even carried one in my handbag. Has a self-capping focal plane shutter, whose speed is controlled by varying the gap between two blinds, the smaller the gap, the shorter the exposure. So great to use as the image is the right way up, only you have to remember it's a mirror image so what you see on the left is actually on the right and so on. You can change the lenses and the lens board itself can be tilted by swinging the geared lever down, which moves the lens board up or the other way depending what you're after.' She sighed with admiration as if she was gazing on an old friend. 'Shutter cloth focal plane, speeds setting of B, 25, 40, 50, 75, 125, 250 & 500th with Aldis Uno Anastigmat 4 inch f/4.5 lens and self-capping.'

She turned back to Nicola and as she illuminated her face she could see that Nicola was as lost and as confused as a child.

'After the exposure the gap between the two blinds closes completely,' Samantha began to explain, 'ensuring that the film is not exposed when the shutter is next cocked and the blinds are returned to the start point.'

'You know a lot about cameras!' Nicola remarked, making Samantha grin.

'I do.'

'Was it a hobby?'

'After I finished school,' Samantha recalled, her thoughts drifting back to happier times. 'Mummy was still a really successful movie actress in Germany and I was at first keen to follow her into the industry. I used to be on set a lot. I had some small acting parts, like the maid, or the street urchin. But for the most part, I worked as a runner, then camera loader and even became a camera assistant and operator. I've come to understand a lot about cameras. I used to take a few photographs on set, and around the clubs and bars of Berlin. The parks, the streets.' She sighed ruefully. 'But I haven't got one at the moment,' adding flippantly. 'Now, of course, it's all America. Was there for a bit as an actress, until Daddy brought me back. Though before then, for a while I did dabble over here on the Isle of Wight, both in front of and behind the camera.' She could see Nicola was impressed as she concluded. 'That's what took me stateside. Great days!'

She swung the lamp back over the counter as they took a couple of paces.

'Had fun with a Bell and Howell.' she sighed.

'At the same time? Must have kept you busy!' Nicola replied.

'Lovely camera.' Samantha mused as Nicola realised Bell and Howell weren't a couple of chaps.

'Oh, it's a camera!!'

They took a couple more paces as they reached the end of the counter and looked for the lifting hatch.

'Aluminium body, nice and steady, easy to crank and has these little pins inside to hold the film steady. Lovely.' Samantha recalled the beauty of the Bell and Howell. 'And a rotating turntable at the front giving the operator four separate lenses! Really nifty.'

'How long were you in the movies?' Nicola asked.

'There? Only for a couple of years, same length of time I worked in pictures in Britain. I only returned back to England last September.'

'Enjoy it?'

'I did.' Samantha sighed. Those times were long behind her now and she knew in her heart they were never going to come back, which, gave her pangs of sadness.

'So why did you stop?' Nicola asked, trying not to sound as if she was prying but she was finding everything about Samantha just fascinating.

'My Daddy thought it was a bit common. He believes there will be a time when absolutely just the most awfully ghastly people will become famous for behaving so frightfully appallingly in front of a camera without no real discernible talent whatsoever!' She sighed as if she begrudgingly agreed with him deep down but had still wanted to do it anyway. 'He believes that any medium which ultimately will debase itself in such a way can only bring about a negative society. Daddy's always been big on society.'

'I see.' Though Nicola wasn't sure she did. Then she noticed she was standing by the hatch and quickly lifted it open. Samantha followed her through and guided them by the bullseye over to a single, plain looking door.

'Could that be it?' Nicola asked.

'Might be,' Samantha replied as she twisted the door handle and they entered.

16

In the streetlamp's half-light, the grey Rolls-Royce silently glided to a halt, its brakes hissing as they bit. The occupants inside were obscured by the shadows. Like a crocodile awaiting its prey, the Rolls-Royce sat there, a few yards back and on the opposite of the street to the Alvis.

A moment passed then a small reddish and orangey glow, the width of a fountain pen, began to radiate deep from within the rear of the car, but nothing stirred.

*

The office was windowless and very small and almost filled by the desk, chair and single filing cabinet so that the door only just opened fully without hitting any of them.

On the filing cabinet there were a number of boxes and above these on a shelf were a number of ledgers, which Samantha proceeded to take down, before turning her attention to the drawers, as Nicola opened the boxes and began to sift through the receipts and invoices, cover notes and credit notes.

On the table there was an anglepoise lamp, which was the only other source of light in the room they were using, angled up so that they could both use the light to see, whilst Samantha used the bullseye lamp to illuminate inside the drawers of the cabinet.

There was nothing she could see in the files that seemed suspicious. They were just the details of his regular customers so she turned her attention instead to the pile of ledgers.

Samantha concentrated hard as she began to leaf through the pages of the sales book. Fortunately she understood what all the items in the title column meant, like fixing fluid, developing fluid, matt and gloss paper.

The rows and columns were neatly written with the sales added up in weekly tallies and with them all added up at the end of the month. Sales and purchases were recorded in a double-entry system, easy to read and understand for her quick and pragmatic mind. She had to admire the minute details and accuracy of the account, as she was able to see, with just a couple of months' tallies, he had a healthy and prosperous business indeed.

'Nothing out of the ordinary with his sales,' she noted, adding with a wry smile as a line caught her eye, 'though he does have a rather large mark-up with his developing fluids.'

At the back of the cabinet and originally obscured by the other boxes, Nicola noticed there was a shoebox, something that seemed strangely out of keeping with the rest of the paperwork, and leaving the invoices alone she took it down.

'What's this?' she asked.

'Receipts probably! Or invoices?' Samantha replied without looking up from a sales book.

'No. They were in a box folder. I saw them earlier.'

Samantha stopped and closed the ledger. She turned to Nicola as she carefully lifted off the lid and peered in.

She was both shocked and surprised. She turned to Samantha and offered the box for her to look at and she was equally surprised.

'Now that's something you don't see every day!!' she remarked as she then reached into the shoebox.

She couldn't believe what they were looking at. It was too hideous, too odious to contemplate, but there they were, staring back at her, defying her sensibilities, her morals as a new, modern woman.

Maybe she shouldn't have been revolted by this, but somehow, because she enjoyed the new freedoms women had fought so hard for, so she could have the fun life she now embraced, this indicated to her that the old guard was fighting back trying to turn time back to when women were subservient.

Was that the way of society? Was there an element that despite progress and change wanted to maintain the evil status quo? To hold others back so that they and they alone could enjoy the richness of life? To deny the very people without whom those riches would be impossible.

The crimes in this box, though not in themselves the weapons to rid her and everyone of their freedom and rights to express themselves, were by their very nature, there to ridicule and objectify to a point by which all would judge the young, free womankind and so seek to hide her back under her medieval weaves.

Reluctantly she suppressed her pride and took a picture out and into the light she could see it more clearly.

It was of a young woman, to her eyes, less than twenty-one years old and with an unknown man beside her, who was lifting her skirt and showing her stocking tops.

She was almost unable to look any more for the image almost made her want to be sick from the very pit of her stomach.

She tilted the image round for Nicola to see and she too was revolted.

'Do you think our Mr Cooke was developing a sideline in risqué pictures?' Samantha asked. 'I mean, this is positively filth!'

'I don't know?' Nicola replied, beginning to rummage through the shoebox. 'So many girls! Hang on a mo!'

She took one out.

'You recognise who that is?' she asked Samantha, who took the photo and looked at the man again and another girl showing off her stockings as before.

For some reason the female face seemed familiar, only she couldn't place it. Same man, but like the first picture, he wasn't looking at the camera. He was slightly obscured, side on, and apart from a small birthmark on his cheek near to his eye, there wasn't really anything of any note about him as far as she could tell, but then she wasn't the sort of woman who noticed men much.

She stared at the picture a little harder, but still she couldn't figure out what she was meant to be seeing.

'No? Should I?'

'Ignore him. Concentrate on her,' Nicola began as Samantha took another look at the picture. 'Take off the hat and the coat and look at the face?'

She looked past the hat, concentrating completely on just the eyes, nose and mouth and then, like an epiphany, she could see it and as she slapped the picture she turned to Nicola.

'That's.... !'

'Mary, yes.'

'Well spotted you!' Samantha was impressed.

'It's a gift; I've always been good on faces.'

Samantha delicately brushed away from Nicola's eyes a hair that had slipped out from under her hat.

'I bet you are!!'

She placed the picture of Mary into her coat pocket.

Suddenly, there was a dull thud, the sound of something falling in the back of the shop.

She quickly turned to Nicola and, with a hurried nod, Nicola turned off the anglepoise lamp as Samantha picked up her bullseye and pointed it to the floor. Together they tentatively went to investigate.

17

Samantha carefully opened the office door, slightly at first so that it wouldn't make a sound, before letting it open out as she peered into the shop. She turned the light from her bullseye lamp tight against her body so the light wouldn't shine and give her away.

She studied the dark shadowy space before her. It was quiet and all she could hear was the sound of Nicola breathing quietly behind her.

In the corner of her eye she noticed it, a shadow, deeper in between two of the free-standing pillar displays in the middle of the shop, as it moved. So without a word, she moved out to behind the counter. Knowing that Nicola was still behind her, she ventured further along the counter, her eyes constantly watching the area that the shadow had moved between.

Strangely she felt very calm. Her mind was too busy concentrating on the shadow to let fear take hold and then as the shadow moved again and came towards them, she paused and waited.

She could tell the shadow couldn't see her as the streetlight only illuminated the front part of the shop and she watched as the shadow began to open a drawer or two as if looking for something in particular.

This was no burglar and suddenly she felt invigorated and empowered. Whoever it was she realised was being furtive because, he was as scared as a fox chased by hounds. Then as the bullseye's light flickered over him, she cried, 'I say. Who's there?'

There was a loud crash as the shadow dropped the drawer, scattering a number of small camera items to the floor. He turned, taking a wild, blind, swing at Samantha. She instinctively dodged it, stepping aside like a flash, as Nicola picked up a nearby tripod and hit the man over his head with it.

Stunned and confused, he fell to the floor holding his throbbing head as Samantha shouted, her chest swelling with pride,

'Attagirl!' And slapped Nicola affectionately upon the shoulder.

She brought the light from her bullseye down onto the man's face. Together they watched him as he rubbed his head twice more before looking up at them both. But all he could see was two figures, black silhouettes and somewhat featureless, towering over him.

'Please, please, please don't hurt me!' He whined as he curled himself up into a ball to protect himself from the rain of blows he expected from this pair of lofty types. 'We were having a bit of harmless fun!' He confessed, hoping they would go easy on him if he could just explain. 'We only took the pictures. I didn't touch 'em like! Please, please you've got to believe me!'

'We're not going to hurt you,' Samantha replied as a steel-like strength echoed in her voice.

'Well, not if you answer our questions,' Nicola added. The tripod rattled as she slapped it like a club into her open hand to emphasize the point.

Samantha glanced back and could just make out a wide cheeky grin and she knew Nicola was enjoying this just as much as she was. The adrenaline rush, the excitement of the unknown, was making her as much alive as she was.

'Bashed by a couple of bearcat flappers!' moaned the man, fearing his day couldn't get much worse.

'It's him!' Nicola suddenly exclaimed.

'Who?' Samantha asked.

'The man in Mary's picture!'

She looked again at the man's face and suddenly she could see the birthmark.

'You really are good!'

'Ab-so-lute-ly.' Nicola replied through her enormous grin.

'So?' Samantha looked back to the man. 'Is that why you're here? Looking for those mucky pictures?'

'It wasn't my idea!' he pleaded weakly. 'It was Cookie. He reckoned we could make some serious dough!'

'And did you?' Nicola asked.

'Not 'alf!' the man admitted, adding, 'You'd be surprised what a price you can get for a mucky picture up Westminster!'

'But?' Samantha encouraged him and, realising he was expected to continued he hesitated then reluctantly added, 'But we never thought it would lead to this! And when I saw you two there, I thought you were the other two fellers who did for poor old Cookie.'

'Well, at a guess, I think it's down the nick for you.' Samantha replied. 'You can tell this to the police and we'll let them sort you out.'

'But I didn't kill Cookie!!' He protested once more.

'I know,' she reassured him, and for the first moment in a long while he began to relax, when suddenly the front window exploded into a thousand fragments as the firebomb bottle crashed upon the hard wooden floor and shattered, spraying the petrol out like a mist in all directions. As the petrol caught the naked flicking fire of the rag that had been stuffed down the bottle's neck, it ignited and the front of the shop erupted in an large, orange wall of fire.

Very quickly thick, choking, black smoke began to billow through the shop. Its acrid smell, as the varnish and cloth burned, began to suffocate them. Quickly Samantha flicked the light around the room looking for the way out.

Then in the glancing kiss of her bullseye's beam, she noticed the glint of the large brown bottles on the high shelves and to her shock she saw how the flames leapt and caught the boxes on the shelves just below them. She realised that in a few moments the flames would be all around those bottles and she alone knew just what those bottles contained.

'Quick, out the back, if those chemicals go, we're in trouble!' Samantha shouted and, grabbing the man, she followed Nicola along the counter as the three of them rushed out of the shop, keeping their heads down as they ran, the flailing fingers of the fire and the confetti of smouldering cinders showering everything around them.

*

They came out of the back door into the yard, Samantha, still holding the man by his jacket collar, and Nicola dived to the cobbled floor as in that very instant, the whole area was rocked as the shop exploded into a huge fireball.

The ripple of the blast, its shock wave, sent glass, metal and wood erupting out into the street and out through the corridor and the back room and out into the yard, showering burning and smouldering rubble all over them, as then the kitchen windows were blown out, and the rear door was shattered and broken off its hinges to fall with a clatter at their feet.

Samantha straightened her cloche hat and sighed with relief. The heel of her shoes were a little scuffed and her coat would need a jolly good cleaning but otherwise she was fine.

She glanced over to Nicola who, apart from a little soot staining her face, which she assumed must be true of her own face too, was all smiles and bright wide eyes, safe and elated as she was. What a girl!

The man moaned, but otherwise he was none the worse for his ordeal and the darkness returned to the yard, the fire within receding back into the shop. Samantha picked up her bullseye, twisted the lever at the top and was surprised to see, even though the glass at the front was now cracked, the bulb had survived and it still worked.

18

The fire began to lick its way around the shop, caressing every object as it felt its way, investigating with its devastating touch to envelop and devour.

After the initial explosions, to survive the fire now had to find a more sustainable fuel and as it did so, it crackled and snapped with delight. Slowly, it would reach its long, stretching, flailing fingers out and detect something new. Then as its heat greeted that new unsuspecting thing, it would show its appreciation with a smouldering glance and suddenly burst into an orange and red heat haze, spreading the fire further and higher as over shattered shelf, collapsed counter and wall as the fire began to grow.

Suddenly there was a hiss and into the black and grey smoke a white cloud of vapour, cold to the touch, came flooding through.

This was something the fire couldn't caress, this was something the fire couldn't embrace, this was something that hurt the fire.

The fire just wanted to live, but this was like acid, causing the fire pain so that it shrank back, seeking solace in the heat and dry but this vapour was cold, this vapour starved it of its oxygen, and the fire cried out as it began to die.

*

A fire pump and crew were fighting the fire, two men were holding a long buff hose with a brass nozzle, which was connected to the back of the red fire engine.

Each man was dressed in black, shiny brass buttons in double rows along his jacket shining as brightly as his large brass helmet, neck guard tightly strapped around the chin.

The engine was long, with seating on each side for four men, with another three able to sit in the open cockpit. The pump was at the rear and the water tank was under the wooden ladder on a rack that ran the whole length of the appliance and which two men were trying to take off as the others ran out two more hoses that were connected to the back of the fire engine, where another man watched the pressure, the water entering the engine from another hose connected to a pipe under a cover in the pavement.

As the engine ran, it drove the pump and the pressure sent a long steady stream of water several yards into the seat of the flames, as the firemen shouted their instructions to one another, the chemicals, film, wood, paper and other combustible items within the shop beginning to burn themselves out.

Fire giving way to smoke.

A little further away, near to where Samantha's Alvis was parked, there was now parked, blocking that side of the street, a police car and behind that a Black Maria into the back of which two police officers were escorting the man, his hands cuffed behind him.

Sergeant Bull and Detective Inspector Warren were with Samantha and Nicola watching the firemen.

Behind them on the corner of the street, its blue lamp still flashing, stood a Gilbert MacKenzie Trench police box, which from behind the small glass windows in its side shone a brilliantly bright, yellowy white light, meaning someone was inside or had at least opened the box, which was big enough for an officer to rest in with a seat and table inside.

'That must have been a nasty experience,' Detective Inspector Warren continued, 'but ladies, you must leave this detective work to the professionals.'

'We would if we could rely upon you to do your work!' Samantha sighed, rolling her eyes, still nursing the burse on her elbow.

Nicola shivered.

'You alright, miss?' Warren asked.

'Just a little cold,' she replied, although he suspected she was really suffering from the effects of shock. She'd never nearly died before and she was still coming to terms with the experience.

'I know what you need.' Detective Inspector Warren turned to click his fingers to a constable standing near the police box. 'Constable.'

The constable crossed over to them and saluted. 'Sir?'

'Constable. Would you give her something warm and strong inside the box.'

The constable saluted again and much to Nicola's bemusement, he led her into the police box.

The Inspector sighed heavily. It was a mess. He could tell there was going to be a lot of paperwork to write up and he was going to have to be creative about it if he was going to make himself look good.

Samantha turned to him.

'By the way, miss, although I won't say it publicly, thank you for finding Cooke's partner for us.'

She smiled with pride.

'You're welcome.'

'Shame no evidence survives.'

'Yes, shame about that.' she agreed.

'But at least we have been able to get a full confession out of him, so at least we can say that there is one less felon on London's streets tonight.' Detective Inspector Warren shoved his hands into his coat pockets, ready to turn away, but he paused as Samantha replied,

'Yes, but although he and Cooke were undoubtedly undesirable types, he wasn't his partner's murderer. There is still a murderer at large out there.'

'I don't know.' He shrugged. 'Give me time. I'll have him confessing to that as well!'

'I'm sure you will. However, I'm more concerned with the truth.' she reminded him.

Just then, Nicola emerged from the police box cradling an enamel mug of steaming tea.

'Nice tea your officers have, Inspector.' Nicola took a sip as she stood beside Samantha. 'And so thoughtful to have some brandy on hand.'

'We aim to please, miss.' The Inspector saluted her, then as he half turned away from them, he added, 'Now if you'd excuse us.' He turned to Sergeant Bull.

'Sergeant.'

'Sir.' Sergeant Bull shuddered to attention and followed.

But as she watched them head back to their police car, Samantha wasn't so convinced. She knew the man wasn't responsible for the fire or for the murder and she was going to prove it.

19

Samantha had a raging hunger. She'd missed supper that night and sat in her purple satin pyjamas at her dining table, eating her cooked breakfast, with next to her plate in a bowl some porridge.

On the sideboard the hotplate warmed the scrambled egg, bacon, sausage, kidneys, tomatoes, mushrooms and in a soup terrine the porridge. She was sure after she had finished this plateful, she would have enough room to go up and have some of each again. Being up all night and having someone nearly kill her, it seemed was a hungry business.

Apart from the long dining table and a cabinet on the other wall to keep the plates and cutlery in, the room was long, somewhat narrowed by the width of the table, and as she sat at the head she could see the street outside through the bow window.

The walls were painted green, a colour that was supposed to aid digestion but, unless she was entertaining, she seldom used this room. There were two large paintings on the two long walls, both of hunting scenes and not at all to her taste. But that was like most things in the house. As she understood it, her Daddy had brought them because they were worth a lot of money. Taste never came into it.

The room on the whole was characterless, but then that was the point, the focus of a dining room was the meal and the company.

There was a gentle creak of the floorboards and Nicola entered the room, in her long nightdress and with her robe loosely fastened about her. She sat in a chair adjacent to Samantha's and yawned slightly. Samantha greeted her with a little warm smile. Even with Nicola's hair a little dishevelled, her skin still so pale with the crust of sleep still in her eyes, Samantha couldn't help but feel a pleasant warmth seeing her and, how delicate she looked. How happy Samantha was to have Nicola sitting by her side.

'Albert's just bringing the coffee and some toast.' She nodded to the sideboard, adding, 'Help yourself to some breakfast.'

Nicola looked behind her and seeing all the food on display, she was at first somewhat overwhelmed. It was more than she had ever seen for Christmas lunch, never-mind breakfast, and there were six in her family.

Though her body wanted to remain in the chair, tired as she was, she forced herself up and decided to help herself, the tempting smell invigorating her from tip to toe as she drew nearer.

She hadn't been hungry when she awoke, but now, she couldn't help herself as onto a large plate she scooped a spoonful of mushrooms, scrambled egg, two tomatoes and a couple of slices of bacon, a kidney and a sausage before sitting down again.

As she unwrapped her napkin and picked up her knife and fork, she turned to Samantha and asked, 'Do you think that, now the police have that man in custody, they will be able to find out who killed Mr Cooke?'

'I hope so,' Samantha replied finishing her mouthful. 'I think that Inspector Warren knows what he's doing. The main thing is, that at last, you were proven right. You did see a murder from the rail carriage and the police will soon have solved the case.'

She ate some more of her breakfast as Albert entered carrying the coffee pot, which he placed upon the sideboard.

'So I thought, as there's nothing more we can do,' Samantha continued, 'how do you fancy taking a bit of a spin out to the park somewhere?' She paused to think as if the idea was a little spontaneous before adding, 'Maybe we could spend the afternoon on the river? Or go to the zoo? It's up to you?'

'Shall I pour the coffee, miss?' Albert asked.

'No, thank you, Albert. We'll do it ourselves. If you could give the Alvis a quick wash before we go out that would be wonderful.'

'Yes, miss,' he replied, and bowed slightly as he left.

'Well?' Samantha asked.

'I was looking out the widow this morning and I did notice it was a lovely day.' Samantha smiled with a joyful twinkle in her eye, as Nicola continued, 'and I was wondering?'

'Yes?'

'Well…. Wouldn't it be fun if we spent the day by the beach?!'

'And how!!' Samantha exclaimed wildly. 'I know a great little lido. I'll get Albert to pack us cossies and we'll be in time for lunch. Then, if you've still got the energy, maybe we could take in a dance too?'

Nicola smiled. That terrible murder and all the worry she had been feeling was beginning to drift away and though she knew she would have to look for a job, she could do that the next day. Today, she was going to have some fun. Then taking a big mouthful of bacon, she began to think of all the wonderful things she would be able to do at the beach.

*

It was mid-morning by the time they were ready to go. Albert had packed them a little lunch that he had placed in a small wicker basket in the boot of Samantha's Alvis and on top of that, he had put her canvas bags, in which he had packed them both swimming costumes and a second change of clothes.

The roof was down and tied off. Dressed in heavy jackets to keep out the wind, skirts that stopped just short of reaching their knees, and contrasting cloche hats, Samantha and Nicola emerged, leaving the front door open behind them.

Albert held open the car door and after they had both climbed in, he closed the door and watched as Samantha started the engine.

As they pulled away, he climbed the steps back up into the house, but as he closed the door, a black, closed top, Talbot Six saloon car began to pull away and followed the Alvis as it turned left at the end of the street.

*

They had been driving for around five minutes down several streets and everywhere the Alvis went the black saloon car followed.

Samantha watched the Talbot Six in her mirror. She couldn't shake that feeling that it was strange that two cars should be going exactly the same way for so long.

She slowed and the black car slowed too, maintaining its distance, and Samantha began to frown.

'What is it?' Nicola asked, noticing she was still watching something in her mirror.

'That car behind us. It's been behind us since we left home.'

Just up ahead of them there was a four-way junction, in the middle of which was a policeman, with his long white gloves and with a white band around his tall dome-like helmet. As they came closer to him, he turned to be sideways to them and holding up his hand, he commanded them to stop.

Samantha took her car out of gear and pulled upon her handbrake, looking back once more into her mirror. The Talbot pulled up close behind them and she could see that inside, two very grim and vicious-looking men were sat staring hard at the back of her car.

She looked quickly at Nicola and could see she was a little concerned before she turned to look back at the policeman and then held her arm out to the right to indicate that was the way she intended to go. As she did so, she checked in her mirror to see the driver of the black saloon car signal right as well.

She depressed the clutch, holding her foot down hard on it, putting the car into gear and keeping one hand on the handbrake and one on the wheel, her other foot hovered over the central accelerator pedal and as Nicola reached out a hand to hold the dashboard, Samantha tightened her grip around the steering wheel, her soft leather gloves creaked gently as her fingers flexed over the highly polished wood.

She glanced to Nicola and gave her a quick reassuring wink and Nicola could see that there was a fiery light shining behind Samantha's eyes as she was gripped by a wicked sense of excitement.

The policeman checked that all the traffic was settled in the other three directions. Then, as he turned to the Alvis and saw it was being driven by a woman, he sighed and with a gentle warm smile he waved to Samantha to proceed.

20

As she let the clutch go, she pulled the release to the handbrake and slid it forward. The brake released and the gear engaged as she slammed her foot down on the accelerator pedal. The Alvis set free like a race horse at the starting line shuddered and rushed forward.

The Alvis's engine squealed as she grabbed the steering wheel tightly, now in both hands, pulling hard at the wheel, hard to the right, round hard, tighter and tighter continuing to turn as she went right around the policeman, making him almost dizzy as the Alvis swung around him, like a shark circling its prey, until it had come full circle. As she straightened the wheel and pushed the accelerator to the floor, passing the back end of the black saloon, that had also moved quickly to follow and was about to turn right, the Alvis roared away down a new road.

The Talbot came to a shuddering halt. There was a loud clanking noise as the driver quickly and a bit too hurriedly slipped the black saloon car into reverse and roared backwards, just missing the policeman, forcing him to jump out the way. The Talbot still turning, slipped into a forward gear and with a jerking bouncing on its springs, raced away down the left lane after the Alvis.

The policeman raised his fist and shook it at them violently as he took his whistle from his left breast pocket and began to blow.

*

Quickly Nicola steadied herself before swivelling around on the seat to look back behind them. The Talbot was behind them but a little distance away.

Samantha was fighting the steering wheel, but she was skilled and competent, in her element driving at speed even if the road was narrow, the cobbles weren't level un-like the track at Brooklands, and the heavy coach spring suspension was not as stiff as a racing car's.

It also seemed to be a little light at the front, but she put that down to the fact that the car was front-wheel drive, not rear-wheel like she was used to and she quickly realised that at speed she was in more danger of understeer than oversteer and had less need to worry about her back end slipping out than losing control of her steering.

'It's still following us!' Nicola confirmed for her, as Samantha hadn't yet had time to look in her mirror.

'Thought they would!!'

'How can we lose them?!' Nicola asked as she swivelled back to hold onto the dashboard.

'Don't you worry, baby.' Samantha replied reassuringly as she patted her steering wheel. Nicola was just confused. 'We've got a straight four, overhead valve, 1496cc, little sports car here and this little girl has all the mod cons, including front-wheel drive, four gears and four-wheel brakes as standard, producing 4500 revs per minute, not bad for a two-and-a-half pint or one-point-four litre engine with a top speed of 75 miles per hour so there's no way they're going to catch us now.'

'But can you handle that much speed?' Nicola asked, as they seemed to be travelling so fast now that the houses either side of them seemed to be passing so quickly that they were nothing more than a blur.

'Of course!' Samantha declared, adding, 'with worm and roller steering. My old Daddy always said it's best with a worm inside, but I'm never sure if he was talking about my cars or not.'

'Quite!' As though Nicola knew what on earth Samantha was talking about.

'I raced for a couple years around the world including the Targa Florio, the Indianapolis 500, the Mille Miglia and Brooklands, all of which I won, though I'm no Dorothy Levitt. But we both raced Napiers! Daddy's got the trophies in his billiard room if you'd like to come down to his country pile sometime and take a look?'

'And how!! But shouldn't we try and outrun these rotters first?' Nicola asked nodding back to the Talbot that was still keeping pace behind them.

Samantha smiled and dropped down from fourth to second gear.

She gripped the steering wheel tightly and pulled it sharply to the right. As she did so, she could feel the back end of the car become light and it slewed out behind them as if it was trying to overtake the front end. She turned the wheel quickly to the left, telling herself opposite lock.

The Alvis slewed almost sideways as it turned the corner, the engine still roaring as Samantha kept her foot on the accelerator. As the Alvis glided over the cobbles and through the bend and as their momentum slowed, Samantha brought the steering wheel straight again. She pushed down again on the accelerator, the engine purring louder, its revs rising, as the rubber of the wheels bit the stone once more and then away they raced down the side street, the revs dropping as she changed up through the gears.

The black saloon car's brakes squealed as it slowed so quickly to a stop, its chassis shuddering as it rocked on its springs. The driver clunked back through his gears to find reverse. The Talbot backed up and then turned to follow the Alvis down the side street.

There were shops and other cars ahead of them now, but the street was still largely empty. Then Samantha spied a space at the kerbside between two delivery carts and slowing quickly with the footbrake, then just before the car came to a stop, depressing the clutch and slipping from first into neutral, the car stopped. Then she released and depressed the clutch again and in the one move, she pulled the gear lever into reverse and as she released the clutch again, with a little touch of the accelerator pedal, not too much but just enough to make the car move, she drove backwards, steering into the space between the two carts and once she was near to the kerb, she straightened up the wheel, then depressed the clutch and pulled the gear lever back to neutral.

She pulled back the handbrake sharply, letting the locking lever go before they both quickly ducked down as just then the black saloon car roared on past.

Samantha peered over the side of the Alvis's body and watched as the Talbot slowed and then turned behind a horse-drawn vegetable cart and headed down another side road.

Then as she slid herself upright again and as Nicola did likewise Samantha depressed the clutch and thrust the car into gear. She released the handbrake and they juddered forwards and as she gave the accelerator a more progressive downward push, the Alvis began to race forward once more and they followed the Talbot down the side road.

*

Coming onto a hill, the Talbot was just in front of them, disappearing over the brow as Samantha went up through the gears, the Alvis getting faster as they closed up.

*

The driver inside the black saloon car noticed in his mirror the Alvis as it came over the brow and quickly he shifted up to top gear and began to push the accelerator down hard too.

*

The saloon lurched forward as the two cars began to race down the hill.

Quickly the Talbot jinked right as it rounded a horse-drawn coal cart. Samantha effortlessly shifted her car to the right as she went past the coal cart.

Then, just as suddenly, the black saloon car slewed under squealing brakes to the left and turned up another street.

Samantha followed as Nicola, trying desperately not to, slid and bumped into her briefly, carried by the momentum.

*

Both cars raced along the street, narrowly missing some metal bins left out front of the houses.

There was the protesting squeal of brakes as the two cars then skidded down a right-hand turn.

*

The passenger of the Talbot held a palm to the roof as he steadied himself and turning to the driver, he looked at him with mild surprise as the driver fought with the wheel, turning it so sharply that the black saloon car swerved wildly as he took it round another corner.

*

They turned again and were racing down the hill. The road was uneven, breaking the hill into two sections, each separated by a minor bit of straight ground and as the black saloon car came over the brow of the straight ground, the driver found himself staring at the rear of another horse-drawn coal cart.

Quickly, he pulled the wheel to his right and slewed the car around the cart, just missing the cart's tailgate and, as the Talbot snaked twice, the driver fought the car back under control and pushing the accelerator pedal to the floor, the front of the Talbot lifted and the car began to race away.

As the black saloon car jinked right, Samantha could suddenly see why and reacting instinctively she turned her wheel left. There was enough room between pavement and the horse-drawn cart and she steered the Alvis for that gap. She could feel Nicola gripping the door and she could sense that her wheels just missed hitting the kerb. As they roared by, the horse whinnied and bucked slightly, but she had her Alvis under control, its engine pulling her to wherever she seemed to point it.

Then as she pulled in front of the coal cart, she accelerated and closed up upon the black saloon car.

*

The Talbot slewed into a side road off the hill. In the mirror the driver could see that the Alvis was still with him, and he suddenly turned the black saloon car right, cutting across another car, forcing it to shudder to an emergency stop.

*

The driver of that car sounded his horn. As the Alvis also cut across him and he beeped again, the driver turning to the two cars that had cut across him and giving them both the two fingers.

*

The driver in the black saloon glanced back into his mirror. The Alvis was still behind them. He had no time to relax, but he had to admire the driver's skill. She was pretty good, especially for a woman.

From off the back seat his passenger took up his double-barrelled shotgun, pushed aside the lever between the two hammers and broke it open. From out of his jacket pocket he took a couple of cartridges, placed them into the barrels and snapped it shut.

With a glance to the driver he patted the stock. The driver returned a slight nod, as he concentrated on the road ahead.

*

She wanted to help, but all she could do was sit there impassively, as Samantha was locked in the chase, focused completely on the black saloon car ahead of them.

*

The road was getting wider and lined with trees on each side. The houses, all semi-detached, had gardens in front of them, with shrubs and bushy plants growing.

All sculptured, nature tamed.

The road now was wide enough for two cars to pass and still allow the cars to come by from the opposite direction.

Both the Talbot and the Alvis were flying by so fast, that they were both passing and catching the other traffic as if they were standing still.

*

Suddenly the Alvis skipped slightly as if one wheel had hit a bump. The car weaved slightly and as Samantha fought with the steering wheel, Nicola slipped against the side of the car and then held onto the dashboard. As Samantha brought the Alvis back in line, they just missed a car coming in the opposite direction.

*

But Samantha didn't slow. The road was now tarmac and like a race track. She was in her element and she was determine to make the black saloon car stop and find out why they were spying on her as she realised, whoever had sent them, must have something to do with Cooke's death.

She put the accelerator down to the floor, the Alvis lurched forward and they began to close right up on the black saloon car.

The road ahead was clear, the houses had petered out and it was largely open ground on their side of the road and so with a quick move to the right and then left with her steering wheel, Samantha had moved the Alvis to the inside. The road began to move into a long sweeping left-hand curve and Samantha began to under-take the Talbot. As the two cars began to come side by side, she started to let her car drift very slightly and, as she expected, the driver of the black saloon car, unable to outrun her, was beginning to drift out wide too.

She turned to look at the black saloon car just as she noticed that the passenger was leaning out of his door, looking back at her and levelling his shotgun at her head.

She swerved just as he fired, missing her, and, as the ring of the shot echoed out, both Samantha and Nicola shrieked.

The Alvis swerved left and right a couple of times as Samantha brought the car back under control. They still had the speed and she was soon back up inside the black saloon car.

The curve was getting steeper now and the Talbot was beginning to edge slightly in front.

The passenger leant out a little. He had the whole of the Alvis's windscreen in his sight and he took good aim.

*

The eyes of the black saloon car's driver began to open wide as suddenly before him, around the corner, came a motorbike, leaning into his direct path.

*

The rider, seeing the car, dropped the motorbike and he and the motorbike slid on towards the black saloon car. The driver pulled the steering wheel violently to his right just in time, missing both the bike and rider, but his passenger lost his aim. He fired but only into the sky as he came crashing back awkwardly into his seat.

*

The black saloon car tried to slow. The driver depressed the brake but nothing happened. He could hear the drums scream their tormented pain as the brakes tried to bite, but the car continued to career out of control, bumping over the opposite kerb.

The steering wheel slipped from his hands as he bounced, hitting his head on the car's roof, and as he quickly tried to take hold of the wheel again, he became gripped with fear as looming before him he could see the familiar column of a petrol pump and behind it, the wooden barn of the garage's workshop.

He wanted to turn the wheel, but it was too late. The petrol-pump attendant threw himself out of the way. The black saloon car smashed through it, sending the post-like pump flying up into the air, as a fountain of petrol spurted up over the car, as it continued to hurtle straight into the wooden shed.

*

There was a loud crashing sound of metal and wood splintering as the black saloon car embedded itself into the rear wall of the barn.

*

From the pipe in the ground, the petrol began to leak and like a river it began to weave its way down the slope towards the wooden barn.

*

Samantha slammed her foot down on the footbrake, the front end of her car shuddered as the four brakes slammed home on her wheel rims and the car whipped slightly to her left, hitting the gravel verge.

Suddenly, before she could correct it, the left-hand side slowed dramatically and uncontrollably. The car began to sling itself around to the left, spinning one hundred and eighty degrees as she turned the steering wheel the other way and desperately tried to stop the car from tipping over.

The air was filled with the dust and gravel grit as into the cloud they spun and then suddenly the engine stalled, the car shuddered and quickly Samantha pulled on the handbrake. As the dust began to clear, Samantha and Nicola turned to each other, their faces etched with shock under the grey dust that clung to the sweat coating their faces.

*

The petrol was beginning to run underneath the black saloon car, like the torrent of an incoming tide.

*

Inside the car, both the men, their faces covered in blood, were beginning to recover from the impact of their crash. The windscreen was completely smashed and tins of grease, oil and paint had fallen in on top of them, partially burying them and as they began to pick the debris off and were cursing to themselves how the oil and the paint had ruined their clothes, the river of petrol crept forever closer and deeper under their car.

Steam was rising from the overheated engine, from the broken radiator.

*

Samantha and Nicola both turned to look over to the petrol station.

*

There was a huge explosion as a massive orange-red fireball erupted from deep inside the wooden barn sending shards of metal, tyre, wood, tins and tools high into the sky.

The fireball erupted around a huge black cloud of smoke that billowed within it. The cloud grew in size and rolled in on itself as if it was trying to devour itself, growing higher and higher into the sky and wider and wider over the petrol station.

*

Quickly they buried their heads below the dashboard as the cloud of dust, dirt, rubble and soot engulfed the Alvis.

21

Samantha was standing by her fireplace, her cigarette smouldering in a long mauve holder as she threw her used match into the cold, empty hearth.

Nicola was sitting in the armchair opposite as behind the coffee table on the sofa sat Detective Inspector Warren, studying closely the notes in his rather worn and battered notebook.

Samantha took a gentle drag and then let the smoke escape effortlessly from the corner of her lips. He cleared his throat, having found what it was he was looking for, and without looking away from his book, he read.

'The two men in the car appeared to be a couple of hoods employed by someone. We don't know who?' He turned to Samantha who just stared blankly at him as he continued. 'To do you both in, miss.'

Samantha shrugged as she took another drag.

'Well, I'm not the kind of girl who's going to let some man do her in, never mind them working in tandem.'

'And there is no way to trace who they worked for?' Nicola asked as she fidgeted slightly with her fingers on her lap.

'By the time the firemen arrived, there wasn't much left of them to identify, miss.' He checked his page again. 'And as for their car, we've been unable to trace it through the number plate as yet. We've a dozen girls at the office looking through the cards, but if it's not from around London, it could take some time to sort out.' He shrugged as Samantha sighed with disinterest. 'I very much doubt you'll have any more trouble today.'

'Thank you, Inspector.' She took the cigarette holder from her mouth. 'But the day's ruined.'

'We were heading for the lido!' Nicola smiled, a little apologetically, still feeling a bit guilty she wasn't working.

'At least we can still go to the Pink Garter.' Samantha added and then took another drag on her cigarette.

'You sure you want to go there, miss?' Warren asked. 'Bit of a dodgy crowd!'

'Yes, Inspector.' Samantha smiled warmly. 'It's Jazz Night.' She really loved her jazz and no one trying to murder her was going to put her off the things she loved.

But it was strange, she conceded to herself, but didn't let the Detective Inspector know, someone somewhere wanted to kill her and for what? She guessed that whoever set fire to the photographic shop had been trying to kill Cooke's partner. That was a reasonable assumption, after all. No one could have known she was going to be there, but Cooke's partner was bound to turn up there at some point if only to recover the photographs. Had she not been there, then probably they would have succeeded but those two in the car? They had been sent to target her and Nicola, or at least Nicola.

She smiled a little secret smile to herself. It was obvious to her, even if it wasn't obvious to the police, that she and Nicola were on to something, that those pictures were at the centre of Cooke's murder and if she was going to solve this mystery, she was going to have to let the photographic evidence lead her back to real killer.

*

In the dark stretching shadows that were filling his office, Barlow sat behind his desk. In his hand he held a glass of whisky. He watched the golden-brown liquid inside through the deep, glinting, crystal sides of the glass, staring into the liquid as if a vision would appear and explain everything to him.

It had all been so simple and now everything was beginning to get rather complicated. He knew he had to take action but what?

He studied the liquid but there were no answers there.

He drank it back in one. Then, as he slammed the glass down on the desk, his eye wandered over to the telephone.

He let the glass go and after a moment's pause, he picked up the handset and flicked the cradle up and down a couple of times. A moment later the operator asked for the number. He gave it and waited as the operator connected him.

The voice on the other end answered. He replied, 'It's me, Barlow.'

He sighed heavily as he could hear the other person berating him.

'How was I supposed to know they would be there?' he pleaded. 'I was just after that other runt!'

He listened to the other person on the phone as they explained the situation to him.

'I did. But...' He was interrupted. 'I know. So now what?' He was told and responded, trying to pass the buck. 'Well, that's your job now, isn't it? So you're not going to do anything about them. Then I'll have to do something about them, won't I!'

He slammed the handset onto the phone's cradle, then he took a cigar from the box next to it and resentfully he lit it.

*

The Pink Garter was a large, three-floor building, central in a row of similar buildings, but with a large canopy over the double-door entranceway and three steps that led up to the two solid, black doors in front of which stood a doorman in a long, grey coat and matching peaked cap. Next to the main door there was a neon sign, with the words 'The Pink Garter' illuminated for all to see and an image of a garter underneath glowing in a bright, salmon pink.

There was a small slip road that ran from the street to the front of all the buildings in that row, just wide enough for a car to run along. A taxi pulled up outside the club and a pair of very fashionable flappers got out. One was wearing a short and all frills green and silver dress with matching shoes, pale green stockings and a sparkly silver and green headband picked out with glittering rhinestones from under which her bright-ginger shingle bob shone like a beacon. Her similarly dressed companion was in blue, with white stockings and a white headband to which was attached a flowing, curving sapphire-blue feather and whose short brown hair seemed a little more unruly.

Samantha paid the taxi driver and placed her purse back inside her matching clutch bag and then arm in arm, she and Nicola both rushed up the steps. The doorman opened the door for them, and with a little giggle and a wink, they quickly trotted in.

*

Across the road, as the bright yellow light in the hallway died behind the closing front door, a small, compact car pulled up in the shadows. Its engine died and the occupants settled down for what they expected was going to be a long wait.

22

After passing the hatcheck girl and another girl with a racy short skirt and a matching smile carrying a tray from a strap around her neck, selling matches, cigarettes and cigars, Samantha and Nicola signed their names in the members book and headed through the double doors into the club room, the space opening out to greet Nicola with a view she'd never imagined possible.

At the far end, under the glare of several spotlights, there was a jazz band on a small raised stage, each musician immaculately dressed in a dinner jacket and a bright white shirt with a black bowtie, playing the fashionable tunes both Samantha and Nicola loved so much.

The room was otherwise shrouded in a shadow of subtle subdued lighting making the tables scattered around the dance floor seem all the more intimate. Each table was laid out to accommodate four, though in some cases two tables had been pushed together to allow a larger party to stay together, and each had a pale red tablecloth and a small pink-shaded lamp in its centre.

The club seemed to be a jumping joint with so many cats beating their gums as they dined.

For Nicola, this club was so liberal. There were chaps dancing with chaps, dolls with dolls and even chaps with dolls. For once, and since such a long time ago it seemed, she really felt she could relax and let the night just happen as no one seemed to care about anything. It made her feel as though there wasn't a care in the world worth getting all hung up about.

The maître d' showed Samantha and Nicola to their table, passing another cigarette girl on their way, and after showing each to their seat, he called over a waiter and left them to attend to the other guests.

Nicola looked around her as Samantha took a menu.

The room had an elaborately ornate ceiling, with low hanging chandeliers of shimmering golden shards against the white circular patterned mouldings, surrounded by a sea of brilliant white, stretching from the ceiling to the top of the walls, where it reached the barrier of the white picture rails that gave way to the mauve papered walls with their fantailed uplighters set around the room at regular intervals. Beneath each light there was a matching fantailed mirror that dropped down to the dado rail and between each mirror around the dining area there was a silver framed poster advertising the joys of the many types of cocktails that were available or of some sunny, distant location in Europe, often depicted by wealthy socialites raising a glass with the name in blue flowing script all around them.

To the side behind Nicola there was a bar, its rainbow-coloured assortment of bottles standing patiently on the shelves illuminated by the lights behind them and as she took her menu, Samantha, smiling like the cat that had got the cream, turned to her and with the exuberance of a child on her first visit to a sweet shop said, 'I've ordered us some drinks.'

Nicola smiled, still overawed by everything. Never once had she been in such a place back in Newcastle. She wasn't even sure a place like this existed there but then she knew it was such a big town that somewhere there probably was such a place, though her father would never have let her find out.

The waiter returned with their drinks, a couple of sidecars, and as he left, Samantha leant over to Nicola.

'I hope nothing shocks you, as after midnight, this place gets a little too liberal for most tastes.'

'Nothing shocks me,' Nicola reminded her, 'I'm from Newcastle.'

'Do you like your sidecar?' Samantha asked. 'Only I can order you something different next time if you wish?'

Nicola smiled warmly as she then took a sip of her drink, refreshing with a warming glow as it slipped down.

'It's the cat's whiskers!'

She grinned as she stared deeply into Samantha's eyes and noticed just how they seemed to sparkle back at her like polished jade and, though she wasn't sure it wasn't the strong alcohol of the cocktail, for a moment she felt a little rush of warmth swell throughout her body and, briefly at least, she felt a tiny bit lightheaded.

Then, as the tune changed, they both looked at their menus for a while. All the different choices, cooked in ways some of which she couldn't pronounce, never mind know what they tasted like, but she didn't want Samantha to think she was overwhelmed by it all. After all, she was here in London to stay and so she was just going to have to get used to all these weird London ways.

After reading and re-reading the four pages over and over again, to Samantha's surprise, Nicola asked,

'Is the steak beef?'

'Ab-so-lute-ly? Why?'

'Well,' Nicola began, trying not to sound too apologetic, almost ashamed. 'Times been so hard back home recently. All you can get to eat in the restaurants is horse!'

She rested a comforting hand on Nicola's.

'Then we'll order two steaks, and what do you say to some apple pie?'

Nicola smiled.

'That'll be nice!'

'This club hasn't been open too long. My friend Harriet introduced me to the place. What do you think?'

'Wonderful.'

They stared longingly into each other's eyes for what seemed like a lifetime and Samantha realised just how light and happy she felt. Just silently looking, a wave of uncontrollable joy seemed to overwhelm her.

It was then that she was suddenly gripped by a gentle tinge of sadness.

Had it not been for the murder of Mr Cooke, although she had found Nicola rather attractive on the train, she would, in the normal course of events, have never spoken to her and yet, in the short time she had known her, she had found her to be the most fascinating and interesting person she had ever met, certainly since she had returned to Britain if not before she had left all those years ago.

She was smart, funny and not just because of her accent, but genuinely witty and intelligent and, although they didn't share the same interests all the time, Nicola as far as she could tell had no great interest in cars, their differences only served to make her all the more intriguing and for a moment she was overcome by an uncontrollable wave of sadness.

She knew, once the murder was solved, Nicola was going to want to be on her way, to find her job and settle down in some working-class area of the city, their paths would never cross again and yet, she so wanted her to always be her friend.

No, that was wrong.

She wanted her to be more than just her friend. She wanted her all and yet, what excuses were there to keep her? She respected her too much to stand in her way, even if it would mean she would lose her for herself and so, as she sipped her cocktail and smiled sweetly looking into Nicola's most adorable blue eyes, that tinge of sadness sat like a halo around her heart.

The waiter came over and patiently waited for a few seconds, hovering at Samantha's side, before both the boredom of being ignored and the fear of losing a tip or three from his other customers, made him politely cough gently in her direction.

With a sense of embarrassment, Samantha turned to him and trying to behave as normal as she felt normal was, she waited as he put his pencil to his notepad.

'Two steaks with chips and two apple pies for dessert.'

He made a note and with a glance from under his brow waited as she added, 'And may we have a bottle of your finest champagne, too.'

He made another note.

'Very good, miss.' he replied, snapping the book shut, taking their menus and going before they could bat an eyelid.

Nicola placed her clutch bag on the table, took her compact from it and checked her make-up in the mirror. It was fine, though she did think her lips needed a little touch up, and so taking her lipstick from her bag, she quickly applied some more to her lower lip before dropping both lipstick and compact back into her bag.

The band was jiving and the sounds were jumping and Samantha could feel her feet tapping to the rhythm. The floor wasn't too crowded and as she turned to Nicola she noticed that she too was watching the band and that her hand was tapping the table in time with the beat.

'Do you dance?'

Nicola turned to Samantha and smiled.

'Are you asking me?'

'Be ab-so-lute-ly copacetic if you say yes? Please? I promise you'll have a gas.'

'Then yes.' Nicola smiled warmly. 'I would love to dance.'

'And how.' Samantha stood holding out a hand to Nicola. She took it and together they walked out onto the dance floor.

As if on cue, the band struck up the fast-flowing strains of a Charleston, the trumpets and clarinet matching the rhythm of the banjos bleating out the chirpy ditty and, as the music took a hold of them both, they let their bodies succumb to the dance and kicked and flicked and shimmered as they began to let their wild, elated joy take them over.

She could feel the ruffles of her dress swish as her body moved and with all this energy and the heat of the other dancers around her, Samantha was sure another dance of such energy would make her glow, but as the dance came to an end, the mood of the music changed and became slower, lighter and restful.

Without a moment's hesitation she felt herself drift into Nicola's waiting arms and as she folded into her embrace they both together began to sway in time with the gentle music.

She felt so soft in her arms, as if she was made of cotton wool stuffed with air, and she felt as if she could just squeeze her and she would become immersed within her. As Samantha pulled Nicola tighter to her, she could feel her little ribs touching hers through her thin dress and feel her breath rise and fall, slipping effortlessly against her. Her sweet, soft breath tingled upon her neck as the glow of excitement set tantalising prickles upon her cheek as Nicola's cheek met hers and it felt to her for a moment that, as she felt her own cheeks blush, they were fused together.

As they swayed, she let a hand slowly glide its way down Nicola's dress, following her sensuous curves, to the small in her back to hover just before it reached her peachy bottom and guided her as Nicola slipped her leg slightly between hers, so that their waists were joined and they swayed slightly together as one.

They were as one and she could now smell the delicate scent of her perfume. It was so perfect, so warming and comforting, when suddenly she noticed that her heart was racing overtime and that she could feel through her dress that Nicola's heart was racing too and yet this was not fear.

This was so nice, so wonderful that she hoped it would never end. She felt so safe and comfortable, more comfortable than she had ever felt in the arms of a woman before, that she never wanted this moment to end. She never wanted to be apart from Nicola and as she folded herself around her, protecting her all the more, she closed her eyes and let the rhythm of the music flow through them both.

The music changed and they stopped. As they moved their heads away, she noticed how her cheek seemed to be stuck on Nicola's and, as they parted, it felt as if their cheeks had been torn from each other's. For a second, they seemed to sting.

She looked into Nicola's eyes and for the first time she noticed that there was a soft grey fleck between the iris and the pupil. For what seemed to be an eternity, as time slowed so a second seemed like a decade, they looked deep into each other's eyes and for the first time in Samantha's life she could see the secrets of the universe and the reason for life staring back at her, like a mirror. The more she saw, the more this knowledge, this sensation, seemed to reflect back to her, making her head spin and her body become as light as a feather blown on a light summer breeze.

They weren't dancing anymore, oblivious to the crowds around them. Sights, sounds, time itself no longer existed, only this feeling, only the life in her eyes.

Then without a word or cue, but as one, as if they knew each other's mind, they kissed.

Softly, with a slight tentative hesitation, their lips touched, so soft they seemed to melt as they touched and as their lips parted, she could feel her lips drop open and as she moved closer again, Nicola did likewise and as their mouths touched, she gently slipped her tongue to roll over Nicola's and with gentle exploring strokes.

Her body tingled and she could feel the electricity surging inside her, leaping in sparks from her body to Nicola's and as an excited shiver shimmered up through her spine, she arched into Nicola and pulled her arms around her as if she could pull her inside and for them to be one.

She never wanted it to end.

*

The grey clouds in the distance were beginning to be touched by the sun as it crept over the roof of the tall buildings that towered over the centre of the city.

The doorman by the Pink Garter sign yawned into the back of his gloved hand and watched as the neon sign near to him went out. It had been a long night and he was looking forward to a nice hot mug of cocoa and a kiss from the wife before going to bed, to do the whole thing again the following night.

His coat with its gold braiding looked quite smart in the daylight and he felt really he should be outside a department store or some hotel rather than this club as no one really got to see just how nice his coat was in the dark.

He could hear footsteps and giggles behind him. He turned and with a small salute as Samantha and Nicola passed him, he was greeted by a couple of cheery waves, which made him smile with pride. He liked it when the guests appreciated his good work.

From across the street, in the little car, the side panel window was unfastened and lowered, as the dark figure inside leant forward so that the muzzle of his revolver extended over the side of the door.

The dark figure took a steadying breath and pulled back the hammer until it clicked for the second time. Taking careful aim, he lined up Samantha between the rear and forward sights and holding his arm with the other hand so his arm wouldn't shake, he tightened his grip around the stock and as Samantha looked up to the miserable sky, which she refused to let dampen her mood, he squeezed the trigger and....

As Samantha leant forward to give Nicola a quick kiss on her cheek, there was a loud crack sound that seemed to shatter the silence of the day. The doorman staggered back two paces, his face contorted as he gripped his chest, the oozing red blood filtering through the gaps of his gloved hands. He then paused and toppled forward, saving himself with a hand on the nearby column. Then, as his body fell limp, he fell backwards into the Pink Garter's entranceway.

The engine squealed and the rubber began to burn as the little black car, shuddering into life, began to race with all its speed away as Samantha and Nicola arm in arm looked once more up at the clouds.

'Someone's running a thick mix, backfiring like that!' Samantha commented as she turned to see the little black car roaring away. 'Must be late for work?' She sighed. 'Now where do we find a taxi?'

23

The taxi pulled away from the front of Samantha's house. The street was quiet and peaceful, curtains remaining drawn closed as most of the other residences were still sleeping.

In her lounge, still dressed in her nightclub clothes and sitting in an armchair, Samantha held a glass of brandy in one hand and the picture of Mary in the other.

Nicola was slouched on the sofa, feeling all sticky, and nursed between her hands her own glass of brandy. She was feeling tired now. She had never been awake for so long before.

A quiet, more restful, instrumental record was playing on the gramophone.

Samantha took a sip and looked at the picture again. She twirled it around with her fingers for a moment and then stopped to look at the picture once more.

'We've overlooked something.'

'Shouldn't we tell the police?' Nicola asked. Samantha quickly replied, 'No.' She took another sip and then lowered the glass to her lap. 'What I mean is, someone thinks we know something which ties them in with the murder of Mr. Cooke.'

'What?'

Samantha shrugged as she thought hard for a moment. It had to be something they'd discovered since they had been to Cooke's shop. The attempt on their lives, everything started then, she reasoned.

'The man in the shop said he thought we were the two who did for Mr. Cooke!' She began thinking out loud.

'That's right!' Nicola replied, sitting up slightly. 'Before he realised we were women.' And then sipped her brandy.

'But he said two.'

'Yes?' Nicola had been surprised at that. He couldn't have known there was two of them there in the dark or with the light from the bullseye in his eyes and she didn't speak until after he'd already said that. He had been expecting two people to be after him, so he had to know who those two were.

'Well, don't you see?' Samantha interrupted Nicola's thoughts. 'That's a clue!'

'Is it?'

'Yes. We're actually looking for two murderers and I think ....' Samantha began to turn the photograph around in her hand as she took another sip of her drink, 'I think Mary might know who they are?'

'Or who hired them?' Nicola added cautiously.

'True.' Samantha shrugged and took a sip of her drink. 'She's our only lead.'

'Ab-so-lute-ly. And how.' Nicola agreed and took a sip of her drink too. Samantha smiled to herself. If she was right, it was all beginning to make sense and if she was right, then she might even know who those two were and how they were always a step ahead of her.

'I wish I was so clever,' Nicola suddenly said feeling a little disappointed. 'Apart from secretarial school, which my father thought would stand me in good stead with a career, I've not had the experiences you have.'

'Privilege brings me my experience,' Samantha replied. She didn't feel Nicola was dim in any way. She just felt Nicola lacked that self-confidence and she knew, given the time to adjust to London life, she would find it. 'When your Daddy owns a syndicate of publications and your mother is big both in pictures and on the stage, one has the advantages of life. One would be unfortunate to squander them.'

'Aha, yes, but you've been a film star! That must have opened the way for you. Made you rich in your own right!' Nicola reminded her.

'My mother's the star!' Samantha took a long sip of her drink and then continued. 'Though I did use to watch her, when I wasn't at school. I was seven when the war broke out, but my career in movies, as an actress, didn't really begin until long after I'd been a racing driver. At the age of sixteen I started making films and as my fame grew, I thought I could make a better career elsewhere. So I went to Hollywood, where at eighteen they put me on a contract.' She smiled to herself as if some very happy moment she remembered but wasn't free to share just yet flashed across her eyes. 'A four picture deal. It wasn't so creative for me as it was back here in Britain, but even so!'

'Still.' Nicola sipped her drink. 'Must have been fun?'

'It was a gas.' Samantha gave a small laugh as she sipped her brandy and recalled to herself just how much fun it was. 'I've been tied to the railway tracks for some handsome hunk to rescue, or in the car pivoting over the cliff edge, or tied to a mast by pirates at sea. But always waiting for a hunk to save me. They only wanted me as an actress because I'd made a name for myself as a racer and they thought the crossover would be good for business.'

'Was it?'

Samantha thought for a moment and stared at her drink, a warm smile stretched across her face as she had to concede, 'Yes, though more so stateside. It was as a director I had my most fun, until the company went bust in '26. That's why I could easily head off stateside, but after that my Daddy didn't want me to do anymore out there. That's why I came back to England at the end of '27.'

'That's a shame.'

Sam sipped her drink.

'Daddy of course gave me a role on one of his papers, nothing too gruesome, just a column on fashion. Hence why I have so much free time.' She paused for a moment then continued, 'But I've always been an independent girl. The only benefit of being in the States was it at least left me independently wealthy. That's why I brought the Alvis. Daddy gave me the Riley. He also gave me this house, the furniture and Albert to chaperone me, but he's no fire extinguisher, I could meet a nice Sheik if I was so inclined. Apart from a couple of other things like my gramophone, most my own money is invested.' She shrugged. 'Daddy's so generous. Why squander what I've worked hard for?' She took another sip of her drink and with a haunted irony she added, 'I'm an independent girl. Well, I have been since they delivered my Alvis!'

'Even so!' Nicola exclaimed in awe of her new friend's experiences. 'That's still interesting. When I was young, all my father and I would do is go around the town, dispensing remedies to those whose ailments predominately appeared to be some sort of fever, either caused by a malady or too much indulgence.' She sighed and looked at her glass of drink, realising that she might need one of those same remedies herself soon. 'I do remember I used to help him prepare the little packets he carried with him in his Gladstone.' She took a sip. 'But really I was never going to be a doctor. Maybe I should have been a lumberjack as I used to like climbing trees a lot in the summer.'

'A right little tomboy, were you?' Samantha asked.

'I think my father really wanted another boy and was disappointed with me when I was born.'

'How could anyone be disappointed with you?'

'If only you knew?' Nicola replied solemnly, sipping her drink.

'Tell me?' Samantha asked softly, her voice almost lost to the music.

'Wouldn't have been so bad, but both my older brothers had good jobs before the steel mill closed.'

'We are all struggling with hard times!' Samantha tried to sound sympathetic, but in truth she knew it wasn't so. She wasn't struggling, her Daddy saw to that, but she hadn't always had it so good, so she knew the pain that Nicola and her family must have suffered and were probably still suffering.

It explained why her best suit had fraying cuffs, why she was shy and nervous of London and why her confidence was so eroded. A hard life, a life of struggle with no end does that to a person, wears them down and robs them and the world of those great achievements they could have otherwise made and strengthened all of society with.

'Some worse than others!' Nicola continued. 'They went out for the full nine days in '26 and were arrested in the riots and since then, they've never really had the opportunities to better themselves.' Nicola took a sip, she wanted to cry, both with sadness and with anger but she wasn't going to allow herself the luxury of either.

'Hard times.' Samantha echoed

'And only getting harder.' Nicola gripped her glass tighter.

'True.'

'My father wanted me to marry, but I could never do that.' For a moment Samantha felt a strange pang of fear flutter through her heart, then with relief she listened as Nicola continued, 'So he gave me his blessing to go and find a career down here in London. As if that will ever happen!?'

'Of course it will!' She tried to reassure Nicola. Samantha put the picture down on the side of her chair and then crossed over to her. 'You're a bright young thing,' she reassured her. 'A doctor's daughter and with a profession in your own right and now living in such a civilised city as London. Only jolly times lie ahead of you now.'

'Once these beastly men are caught!' Nicola replied.

'Yes, then it will be the cat's meow for you!' Samantha agreed.

'For me!' Nicola didn't believe it.

Samantha gently placed her hand upon Nicola's knee and with a coy smile and heartfelt gusto, she replied, 'You're the cat's pyjamas,' which took Nicola aback. 'You're so wonderful. I'm so glad you were born a girl. I don't think I could bear it if you weren't!'

'You're just saying that!' Nicola replied, her negativity trying to win through.

'No, I'm not. If I may be so bold.....' She looked Nicola right in the eye. It was time to bite the bullet and regardless of the outcome she felt she had to say it and just accept the consequences. 'I'm rather stuck on you.' And she waited with bated breath.

'You're stuck on me!' Nicola exclaimed. Her head was spinning but it wasn't the alcohol. She was confused and elated at the same time and she felt her whole body tremble with excitement and fear. 'But you're so rich!' She was still surprised as after all she herself was so poor. 'You must have the whole of polite society to choose from?'

'The problem with polite society is, it often isn't,' Samantha remarked.

'I see.'

'And much as I have my racy past, if I'm on the level, deep inside of me, I'm just like any other Jane, baby. I'm just looking for someone to have a goofy time with and I just so much want to be goofy with you.'

She had said it. There was nothing more she could do. If the Pink Garter hadn't been a dream, if what she believed she had felt was real, now was the time to know for sure. It seemed to be an age, but she waited as Nicola ran all this through her mind.

'And how! And I so ab-so-lute-ly want to be goofy with you.'

They looked into each other's eyes for a second or three, but just as they began to lean in and kiss, the door opened and, as they both quickly parted, as if they had almost been caught doing something a little mischievous, Albert entered.

'I've turned the beds down, miss, and have placed your water bottles at the foot of your beds.'

Samantha cleared her throat. 'Thank you, Albert.'

'If that's all, miss, I'll retire for the night?' He ended with a question as the beaming sun broke through the curtain and he realised more accurately he should have said 'morning', but he too had been up all night and was beginning to feel too tired to care.

'That will be all,' she replied. 'I think at any rate, we should be getting to bed too. Don't you agree, Nicky?'

Nicola looked embarrassed as tongue-tied she tried to find a something to say.

'Yes, that's right,' Samantha continued. 'We've got to see a woman about a photograph.'

24

Barlow puffed on his cigar as he stared hard at his telephone. The hard black plastic, shone lifelessly with the light from his desk lamp falling upon it as if it was a precious stone and yet, like everything he had held dear, everything about it was false, just an illusion.

He place his cigar on an ashtray and after a moment's hesitation, he picked it up and asked the operator to connect him with a number that he had written on a piece of paper he had by the phone.

The voice at the other end answered.

'They were lucky!' he told the voice. 'That's all. Like I said, if you can't do anything, then I'll do it myself.'

He listened to the voice but the more the voice said the less inclined he was to listen. It was all getting too much for him now and he wanted it resolved.

'Then it's time you got off the fence and got your hands a little dirtier, eh?' He forcefully let the voice know how he felt. Then, as he listened indignantly, his patience snapped and he interrupted almost exploding with anger.

'Oh, oh, oh, you think so, do you? You just remember in whose pay you are and why! I'll meet you at the usual place.'

Reluctantly the voice agreed.

'Good, so we're settled.' And Barlow hung up.

He picked up his cigar and took a couple of puffs, pausing only when there was a knock at his door.

'Come in.'

The door opened and, holding some letters, there stood Mary. She smiled as she brought them over and placed them down before him on his green desk blotter. He looked up at her as she was about to walk away. So innocent she looked and so young.

'Mary?'

'Yes, Uncle?'

He paused for a moment as if he was about to say something, but somehow, those words just didn't seem to come to his lips and so, shaking his head, he gently muttered. 'Just popping out for a while.' He paused to look along his desk once more to his phone and sighed ironically. 'If anyone calls round for me. Tell them..., tell them I'll be back by one.'

She nodded she understood and left him. He watched the door shut and the room was quiet but for the sound of the clock. Then he slid open his bottom desk drawer and, after moving a couple of papers, he revealed his old army service revolver.

Carefully, he took it out and after closing the drawer, held the gun aloft in his hand and examined it. He kept it well oiled and clean. He broke the chamber open. Inside the drum, six bullets were loaded ready.

He snapped the gun closed and checked that the safety catch was on.

*

As Barlow roared away from his factory's yard in his car, from the other direction Samantha and Nicola in the little Alvis gently rolled in, parking in Barlow's own personal parking bay.

*

Merrily Mary typed away at her desk, her fingers flying over the keys instinctively, without her having to look she pressed down key after key, in such a blur, it was hard to see what keys she touched. She sat there, with her head turned away from the carriage, reading the notebook at her side and turning the squiggles and lines into letters on the crisp sheet of paper that rolled up each time the carriage was slung back to the start by Mary pushing the long chrome lever at its left end back to the right as far as the carriage would go.

As the door to her office opened, she looked up cheerfully and was a little surprised but still pleased to see Samantha and Nicola coming in.

'I'm sorry, but Mr Barlow is out at the moment. You've just missed him.' She smiled, but as Samantha then tossed the photograph down before her and she saw just what it was, she became gripped with a deep, icy terror. She trembled with fear and with absolute disbelief that it was all happening like a living nightmare, the shame, the embarrassment. Her bottom lip quivered as she wanted to cry.

'Oh my God!!' She felt faint. 'Where did you...!!?'

'From the guy who took this shocking picture,' Samantha replied dourly. 'And before the guy in that picture could destroy it.'

'Oh my God!!' She tried to cover her lips, but her hand shook too much.

'I believe the man who took this picture was murdered by a person or persons known to you,' Samantha continued dominantly, leaning over poor Mary slightly, crowding her so she couldn't flee. 'Who knew what those perverts had done to you? And anyway, what these men did to you was wrong. Justice has to be that of a court of law. Murder can never be allowed to be its substitute.'

'No. But...' Mary stammered as the tears welled up in her eyes. 'Why are you talking to me?'

'Did you ever tell anyone about... this?'

Mary was shocked. She had always considered herself a good girl but a picture like this would always taint her reputation if it became public knowledge even if she had been fooled into it.

'You see, he tricked me.' She dabbed a tear away from her eyes. 'We met in a pub. I was only there to pick up a couple of bottles to take out, you understand? When, when he said he knew this chap down the park who sells capsules of coke two for a shilling, well, it seemed like a buzz, so I thought, why, what the hell! I wasn't to know he had a friend and that they were going to, going to take horrid pictures of me and sell them to their friends.'

'So who did you tell?'

'As his private secretary I am the face of my Uncles company and... and... images like this, the company's reputation and all!'

'Who?' Samantha demanded.

'I... I had to.' Mary's resistance gave way. 'I... I confided in my Aunt.'

Samantha turned triumphantly to Nicola.

'Mrs Barlow.'

'Who was bound to tell Mr Barlow!' Nicola grinned as Samantha turned back to the now crying Mary.

'Where is Mr Barlow now?'

'Today?' She composed herself and dried her eyes. 'Well, he has gone off to see a couple of his old Army comrades from the War. They were all at the Battle of Ypres together and on this day, once a month, they pop along down to the Old Elephant to raise a glass in memory of those at the battle who didn't come back.'

'Who does he meet?'

Mary blew her nose in her little handkerchief.

'I don't know!'

'So where's the Old Elephant?' Samantha asked.

'Empire Street.' Mary replied. 'Down the docks.' She sniffed back a couple of tears. 'It was where their old regiment met before they embarked on their way to Belgium.'

25

As they left the factory building and started to head back to the Alvis, Nicola was feeling a little pensive. She knew dockland areas could be pretty rough places and turning to Samantha she asked tentatively so not to make it seem she was being overcautious, 'Do you know where the docks are from here?'

'Oh yes,' Samantha replied casually, as if she'd spent all her life there, or wasn't aware of the danger which made Nicola all the more nervous on her behalf, 'but first, we have to make another call.'

They climbed into the car and soon had driven across town to Scotland Yard.

Scotland Yard was along the embankment, near to Parliament. A four-story, red-brick building, with every few yards a white course of bricks dividing each red section and with its tall windows and Dutch-style roof of a bell-like gable end and with a tower in one corner topped off with grey slate tiles, it was a large and imposing building in a street of otherwise tall, grand, white neo-classical, Greek-style office buildings.

Samantha drove her little car along the front of Scotland Yard and through a set of gates that divided the two similar, mirror-imaged buildings that made the one complex and along the drive and under an arch of a covered bridge that joined the two halves together before coming to a parking bay at the back reserved for visitors.

They were shown along the labyrinth of corridors to the office and the man they wanted to meet. After some time, as they were leaving that office, they saw Detective Inspector Warren coming out of his, further along the corridor.

'Miss Bishop? Miss White?' He was taken aback. 'May I ask, what are you both doing here?'

'Come to see you really.' Samantha replied.

'But this is my office,' he replied, pointing to his own, realising that they had come from somewhere past his, from inside the building and had obviously been seeing someone else.

'I know,' she replied. 'I was just popping in to see a friend of Porky's on the way.'

'I see?' He was a little suspicious, but then, busybodies always made him feel that way.

'Anyway, we're glad we caught you,' Samantha continued.

'You are?'

'Yes. Only, we believe we know who killed that photographer chappie, Mr Cooke.'

'Oh? Yes?' he replied warily as Samantha continued.

'Yes. We believe Barlow killed him because of some pictures he took of his ward and we know where he's going to meet the men he paid to do the killing for him.'

'Where?' Warren asked.

'The Old Elephant.'

'Know it.' He closed his office door. 'I'll just find Sergeant Bull. I'll meet you down there.' He watched as Samantha and Nicola walked away, his hands twitching as he nervously wondered what he should do next.

26

The Old Elephant Pub was a tall slim, three-story, yellow-brick building in a row of similar properties, distinguished from the others as it was on the corner and had its ground floor windows etched with the brewery company's logos. On the corner there was a large, double entrance over which hung the pub sign of an elephant facing out to the street and a gas lantern. There was a step up into the building which was bowing were it had been worn away by the decades of almost constant use.

Most of the other buildings were houses and the two floors above the pub were both the owner's accommodation and rooms that were let to the passing sailor trade. The cranes on the nearest wharf stood high over the row of houses opposite like some iron giants keeping an eye on the people who lived there.

The street was full of the sounds of the wharfs at work, heavy machinery clanging and clattering as winches lifted the heavy cargos of sugar, iron ore and wood from the boats in dock, leaden clouds of smoke rising above it all, mixed with the stench of petrol and coal which drifted on the air and gave it a grim metallic smell.

In the street there were a few cobbles missing and there was rubbish collecting around the kerbstones. A rag and bone cart, its horse struggling against the incline, made its steady way up the slight hill, its driver shouting for rags as they passed, pausing only to gather any willing contributor's bundle.

Samantha's car pulled up in front of the pub, right on the corner, and as the engine died, she followed Nicola out and together they stood on the pavement, looking at the pub, with a sense of foreboding.

They looked at the two doors, one marked Saloon, the other Lounge.

'Which bar do you think he'll be in?' Nicola asked taking a steadying deep breath as she noticed that some of the red paint was peeling away from the doors and that there was a crack in one of the lamp's glass panes.

'The lounge,' Samantha replied. 'Can you imagine Mr Barlow rubbing shoulders with the working class!'

They entered the lounge bar as across the road and few houses up, the police car with Detective Inspector Warren and Sergeant Bull pulled to a gentle stop.

*

The lounge was a cramped space. Dominated by the bar that ran through to the saloon, the rest of the space had been filled as best it could be with a number of small round tables around each of which there were four chairs and each table had in its centre a small metal ashtray, most of which were in need of emptying.

By the windows, the tables were rectangular with long benches either side and a half wall behind as if to isolate each snug from the one next to it. On top of the divide between each bench, there was an etched glass panel, matching the windows. As Nicola and Samantha looked around the room, Nicola noticed in one of the snugs Barlow was sitting all alone, with a half pint of beer he was cradling in his hands. He looked at his watch. She nudged Samantha gently with her elbow, as she glanced to the clock behind the bar, it was just coming up to midday and, as Samantha turned to her, she pointed to Barlow and together they made their way over to him.

He looked up and sighed heavily to himself as he saw them approach.

'Miss Bishop! How?'

'I asked Mary.' Samantha replied.

He nodded and gave himself a wry smile as he could just imagine Mary being so helpful. But then that's why he had done what he'd done.

'And to what do I owe this pleasure?' he asked, but he knew why as soon as Samantha tossed the photography of Mary before him.

He sighed heavily, resigned to his fate.

Behind her, Detective Inspect Warren and Sergeant Bull entered, letting the lounge door swing shut behind them.

Barlow picked up the photograph and then shuddered with shock as the image of his niece and the abuse she must have suffered to have revealed herself in such a compromising way sickened him to his core. He'd seen images like this many times when he'd been in the army, but knowing her, her being family made the atrocity smart so deeply. If she had been some working-class girl he'd never met, then maybe he could have turned a blind eye, but his niece? Never.

'How did you?' he asked.

'We found it at the photographic shop you burnt down,' Samantha replied curtly. Barlow was shocked.

'I... I... I...' he stammered just as Detective Inspector Warren and Sergeant Bull arrived to stand behind Nicola and Samantha.

'Let me see, and correct me if I make a mistake, Mr Barlow,' Samantha began, 'but I think this is how and why all this happened.' Barlow took a nervous sip of his beer, spilling a few drops onto the table. 'You're a well-respected and successful businessman and a pillar of our society, who, since his brother's death, has undertaken the role of guardian to his brother's daughter. For nearly 13 years you've looked after and cared for his daughter as if she was your own, until you've come to look upon her as your own.' She paused to watch his eyes and she could see in his furtive glances that she was right. 'So what must have gone through your mind when such pictures came to your attention? Not just the scandal of such intimate pictures of your niece being on sale, compromising her modesty, but with her still being under twenty-one, still a child, the scandal was all the more acute!' Samantha continued. 'And so, with a little investigation, you discovered who was selling these images and who was creating them and you took it upon yourself to meet with this man, Mr Cooke, as we now know, late at night in your office.'

'Very good so far, Miss Bishop. Pray continue,' he replied. Much to Samantha's surprise he now seemed much more relaxed as if all his fear had gone.

'So what happened?' Samantha asked. 'Did he refuse to hand over the negative, threatened to sell more copies? Did you discover then that he was doing a roaring trade in mucky imagery?'

'You tell me!' Barlow shrugged.

'I suspect the conversation got heated,' she replied. 'I doubt a man like yourself met him alone, if only for your own safety, so what happened? A fight broke out and what? He accidentally got himself thrown through the window? A problem and, if an accident, a long prison sentence at least would follow and you couldn't protect your Mary from inside Dartmoor. So what did you each agree? Did the others go and hide the body, whilst you made arrangements to fix the office window? It wouldn't have been hard for a fellow like yourself! What with your connections through the Chamber of Commerce, not to mention I suspect, you're a Mason too! It wasn't hard to call in a few favours and have the work carried out that same night. Even if Mr. Cooke's death had been unexpected, you are a man of such organization, it wouldn't have been long until you had everything under control again, but there was one thing you couldn't control, wasn't there? The one thing you overlooked.'

'Go on,' he encouraged her, as he sipped some more of his beer.

'That my very good chum here, Miss White, would see the murder from the railway carriage and that we would persist in our quest to discover the truth.'

'True,' he admitted.

'You torched the photographic shop to get rid of the evidence.' Samantha challenged.

'True,' he admitted again. 'I knew that there were other pictures, Mr. Cooke admitted as much and the other man, the one in the photograph, would turn up at some point to retrieve them. So I had the place watched and so waited until he was inside. I didn't know you were there.' he added. 'I swear.'

Detective Inspector Warren and Sergeant Bull drew their truncheons ready.

'But he lived and you realised that shortly,' Samantha reminded him, 'we'd find the answer and discover that you were the real man behind Mr. Cooke's death.'

'I couldn't take the chance,' Barlow continued, 'so I hired a couple of goons to take care of you.'

Suddenly Detective Inspector Warren and Sergeant Bull swung their truncheons, hitting Nicola and Samantha on the head, sending both the girls sprawling unconscious over Barlow's table as he lifted his glass so they didn't spill his beer.

'Though, of course,' Barlow grinned smugly, 'they were not the same guys with me that night. To get away with murder, it's handy to have a couple of sympathetic police officers who can amend the evidence as desired to help one cover one's tracks.'

'What we going to do with them now?' Warren asked.

'My car's round the back.' Barlow continued earnestly. 'I have a Mason pal up Shepherds Bush way who runs Ramsbottom's metal smelting plant. We'll take them there.'

27

The high brick walls with their barbed wire glistened in the half light of the green glowing gas lamps along the dirty, rundown street. There were oil drums and other rubbish spread all along the street up to the huge nine-foot high, double wooden gates with the name Ramsbottom's Yard in peeling paint over the two halves.

The night was dark and the yard's large chimney, in silhouette, poured out its thick black smoke into the still air.

Barlow's Rolls-Royce, followed by Detective Inspector Warren driving the Alvis and the police car with Sergeant Bull, drove through the gates and into the yard.

Some ten or so of Ramsbottom's lorries stood in a row, to one side of the yard, and on the other the large mounds of metal rubbish, piled like a mountain range, led around to the back of a wooden hut that greeted them.

This was a few yards in front of the austere, almost featureless, red-brick factory that nestled around the base of the huge chimney and was lit by a number of smaller gas lamps attached to its outer wall, giving the building a shimmering green halo around its centre and lower half.

The three cars stopped outside the hut and quickly both Sergeant Bull and Detective Inspector Warren rushed to the Rolls-Royce, Sergeant Bull fetching a flat barrow on his way. Barlow stepped out and entered the hut. Sergeant Bull, as Detective Inspector Warren held the door open for him, lifted in turn Nicola and then Samantha out from the back seat and onto the flat barrow and wheeled them into the hut.

Barlow closed a cabinet as they entered and in his hands he held some twine, which he and Detective Inspector Warren then used to tie Samantha's and Nicola's hands and feet together.

As the others waited, Barlow left the hut and crossed over to the factory to return a few moments later.

'All's clear,' Barlow assured the other two. 'We can take them into the factory now.'

Detective Inspector Warren held the door open for Sergeant Bull to push the barrow out and, after waiting for Barlow to follow, joined them outside.

Sergeant Bull pushed the heavy barrow up the small incline, gasping slightly as he found it hard work. Detective Inspector Warren and Barlow followed.

*

The factory opened out into the huge furnace room, where six large, brick, blast furnaces with huge iron doors, their fires raging inside, smelted down the metal, fed into them by huge hoppers.

It was a cathedral of pipes, coal, metal and brick with the deafening noise of the blast furnaces' roar ringing in their ears.

Sergeant Bull pushed the barrow over to a nearby furnace as Barlow and Detective Inspector Warren followed. Turing back to them, he shouted, 'Now what?'

'Put them in the furnace,' Barlow ordered him as Sergeant Bull, hesitated.

It was then that Samantha opened her eyes and looked over to Nicola.

'You awake, baby?' she whispered to her, as then Nicola opened her eyes and smiled.

'Push 'em into the furnace?' Sergeant Bull asked, still unable to comprehend the order he'd been given.

'Aha,' Barlow nodded eagerly. 'That's a good man.'

'Look, sir.' Sergeant Bull protested. 'I don't mind tampering with evidence, lying, cheating and roughing up a couple of girls, but it wasn't me who shoved Cookie through the window. That was you two! I'm only guilty of aiding and abetting. It's you two who's up for the rope, not me!'

A sudden gunshot rang out over the overpowering din of the furnace as Sergeant Bull, holding his stomach, looked rather surprised as his blood began to ooze out over his fingers. He gasped trying to say something, but before he could, he fell to the floor dead.

'I hate bent coppers who suddenly develop a conscience,' Barlow sighed holding the smoking revolver in his hand.

'Now what we going to do?' Detective Inspector Warren asked.

'Chuck him in the furnace with the two girls!'

Detective Inspector Warren shrugged to himself and then picked up Sergeant Bull's police helmet.

'Sheba,' Samantha whispered. 'Can you reach into my top jacket pocket for me?'

Nicola nodded gently as her hands reached up to Samantha's pocket.

Barlow picked up a dirty cloth and using it to shield his hand from the heat of the iron door, he pushed up the lever and opened the furnace. A wave of warm air almost suffocated him as Detective Inspector Warren threw Sergeant Bull's police helmet in. It felt so hot that he could almost feel his skin being flayed from his bones.

The hat caught fire and was virtually vaporised before it even touched the molten metal within.

'You'd better put Bull's body on top of the girls and push them all in together,' Barlow advised him as Warren turned away from the heat.

'Why me?'

'I'm the chief executive of an international company,' Barlow replied indignantly. 'You can't expect me to dirty my hands with manual work now, can you?'

Detective Inspector Warren sighed heavily.

He nodded towards Sergeant Bull's body. 'Well, you can at least help me get his body on the barrow. I can't lift it on my own.'

Reluctantly, Barlow sighed as they then both crossed over to Sergeant Bull's body.

28

She slipped the long, slim Metropolitan Police whistle out of the pocket and holding it up to Samantha's lips, Nicola held it steady as Samantha took a deep breath.

As Detective Inspector Warren and Barlow picked up Sergeant Bull's limp body, Samantha blew and the sound of the shrill police whistle echoed out over the harsh sounds of the crashing and roaring furnaces. Before Detective Inspector Warren or Barlow could react, from the entranceway and the other various doorways, down the metal stairways and rushing all along the vast cavern of the furnace room, dozens of police officers, all with their truncheons drawn descended upon them and started to hit Warren and Barlow repeatedly, raining blow on blow as

Detective Inspector Marriot arrived in the main entrance doorway with his assistant, Sergeant Finch, at his side.

After taking stock of the situation, he quickly rushed over to the flatbed barrow and hastily began to untie Samantha's wrists.

'Looks like your little ruse worked!' he commented, rather impressed.

'Of course!' Samantha replied rubbing her wrists before untying her own ankles. 'Thanks to Nicky, that is.'

Nicola smiled proudly as Marriot untied her wrists.

'I'd say!' he agreed, astonished. 'Who would have thought of putting on two cloche hats with a copper disc padded with leather to protect your heads from the blows of truncheons?'

'We realised that the only way he could be one step ahead of us at all times was because he had the help of the police,' Samantha began, 'who themselves were unable to follow the same clues we had to follow! Then we were sure that they both had to be in on it too.'

'And we knew,' Nicola added as she unfastened her ankles, 'that if they knew we knew how it was done, then they would have to act too.'

'Then, having me have my men flood the Old Elephant,' Detective Inspector Marriot continued, 'pretending to be customers and eavesdropping on your conversation with Barlow, was a masterstroke. Once we knew where he was going to take you, and with my Sergeant, Finch, shadowing you to make sure you were safe, we were able to ready our little trap. Catching them in the act.' He puffed out his chest with pride. 'Your plan worked perfectly. That was so clever of you both.' he agreed, adding, 'You being women and all!'

Samantha turned to Nicola.

'Attagirl,' giving her a conspiratorial wink.

'Take them away,' Marriot ordered his men as they stopped beating Detective Inspector Warren and Barlow up and then the police officers led them both away.

'Oh, before I forget,' he turned back to Samantha, 'give my regards to Porky when he gets back and I'll see him next week at the Temple.'

'I will and you give my love to Claire.' Samantha added.

He sighed ruefully, and then he gave them both a sort lax salute before leaving them both sitting on the flat barrow.

29

Samantha and Nicola were soon driving back and it wasn't long before they entered Samantha's street, pulling to a stop outside her house. Samantha turned off the headlights and, they left the little sooty, dusty Alvis and swiftly went inside.

After quickly cleaning up, they went down to the lounge. Samantha sat in her armchair with Nicola on the sofa. Albert entered with a tray all laid out with tea for two, which, after he had set it down, he proceeded to pour.

'Albert.' Samantha spoke as he handed her a cup of tea.

'Miss?' She took it and he then handed Nicola hers.

'The Alvis will need a clean tomorrow. I rather foolishly left her for a few hours down by the docks and with the soot from those smelters' chimneys, well, she's not really looking her best. Will you check she's still running alright. Make sure the carburettor's not too clogged up. I'll use the Riley tomorrow.'

Nicola took a sip of her tea.

'Yes, miss.' he replied.

'Now all this beastly business is over, I suppose I had better pack!' Nicola said rather solemnly.

'There's no dickey on the Riley, miss,' Albert reminded her. 'You could put the mistress's bag on the rear seat, or let me attach the box to the rack. Or you could wait until after I've inspected the Alvis?'

'No, that's alright, Albert.' Samantha put her cup down.

'Miss.'

Samantha turned to Nicola.

'What do you mean? Pack?'

'I can't stay here forever,' Nicola replied. 'I have to find a job, a flat of my own!'

'But I have plenty of space here!?' Samantha insisted.

'I know, and your hospitality has been much appreciated. But what reason can I have to stay?'

'We have fun, don't we?'

'Fun's great,' Nicola agreed, 'But I can't stay here with you, just for fun!?'

'Then stay with me for the adventure,' Samantha asked. 'We make a good team, don't you agree?'

Albert went in front of them to start stoking the dying fire. Spring might have sprung, but there was still a chill in the air at night.

'The adventure?' Nicola asked quizzically. She wanted to stay but what other adventures could there be?

'Yes.' Samantha smiled warmly. 'You and I could find a lot of fun things to do together, don't you agree, Albert?

'If that's what you wish, miss?' He responded, but then he was only employed to look after her. What she got up too was no business of his.

'It's tempting.' Nicola agreed. 'But what about my room?'

'You can have the spare. You don't mind looking after two women, do you, Albert?'

'No, miss, though it will mean double the laundry. Especially the bedding.' He shrugged.

'Then she can move in with me.' Samantha replied. My bed's a double and I've got plenty of wardrobe space.'

'I..... I don't know what to say.' Nicola was overwhelmed.

'Have a drink.' Samantha encouraged her. 'Think about it.'

'I....'

'You in a hurry to go?' Samantha asked.

'No?'

'I find life's a lot better with two.' Samantha smiled.

'I don't know what to say!!' Nicola beamed happily.

'It would be so swell,' Samantha continued, 'and anyway, how can we be goofy together if you're living on the other side of town? Just say yes and be my girl!'

'Yes. Ab-so-lute-ly.' Nicola agreed and Samantha squealed with delight. She crossed over to Nicola as they warmly embraced each other so tightly they felt as if they would explode.

There was a knock at the front door and Albert left to answer it.

'Since we danced at the Pink Garter, I've been dreading the end of this beastly business as I feared you wouldn't want to stay.'

'And I thought, now it was all over, that you would want to get back to your society and forget all about me.'

They embraced once more then as they were about to kiss, the door opened and Albert entered, holding an envelope in his hand.

'Sorry to disturb you both, miss. Only there's a telegram for you.'

Samantha reluctantly let Nicola slip from her embrace and crossed over to him.

'A telegram?'

'I paid the boy sixpence, miss.'

'Then help yourself to sixpence from my purse,' she took it from him. 'I wonder who it's from? Can't be Daddy, he won't be back in London before the clocks go forward.' then she opened it.

Nicola watched her with a little nervous apprehension hoping that it wasn't anything serious, when suddenly Samantha cried out with an ironic laugh.

'Why, it's Porky.'

'Miss,' Albert sighed, 'shall I order the extra drink now or wait until after his visit?'

'After I think. We don't want to encourage him,' she turned to Nicola. 'He says, he has some spiffing wheeze and wants to know if I want to join him in it. He's going to tell me what it is when he arrives.' she grinned as Nicola looked bemused. 'I wonder what it could be?'

Albert sighed and rolled his eyes as he left the room. It looked like life was just going to be a little more intense.

THE END

ABOUT THE AUTHOR

Anthony Day was born in Margate, Kent and now lives in
Whitstable writing contemporary, science fiction, fantasy
and historically based fiction.

www.ingramcontent.com/pod-product-compliance
Lightning Source LLC
Chambersburg PA
CBHW072124170626
46813CB00004B/1679